Metaphorosis

June 2018

Beautifully made speculative fiction

Also from Metaphorosis Books

Reading 5X5: Readers' Edition
Reading 5X5: Writers' Edition

Best Vegan Science Fiction & Fantasy

Best Vegan SFF of 2017
Best Vegan SFF of 2016

Metaphorosis Magazine

Metaphorosis: Best of 2017
Metaphorosis: Best of 2016
Metaphorosis 2017: The Complete stories
Metaphorosis 2016: Nearly Complete Stories
Monthly issues

by B. Morris Allen

Susurrus
Allenthology: Volume I
Tocsin: and other stories
Start with Stones: collected stories
Metaphorosis: a collection of stories

Metaphorosis

June 2018

edited by
B. Morris Allen

Metaphorosis Books

Neskowin

ISSN: 2573-136X (online)
ISBN: 978-1-64076-110-0 (e-book)
ISBN: 978-1-64076-111-7 (paperback)

June 2018

The Foaling Season

Samuel Chapman

Reynard aux Chatillon delivers a gryphon foal the morning Lucia Camoreux comes to visit. It comes out squealing, eyes shut and wings folded, sticky with placenta. Within an hour its wings open, beating softly, as it stands to take food from its mother's beak.

Reynard sees Lucia as he returns from leading the foal and mare into a paddock isolated from the pasture. The mare cannot be kept from flying, of course, but she will return to the smaller enclosure as long as her flightless child is there. She will lick its wings so she can always pick it out of the herd. In twenty-eight hours, she will boost it into the air for its first flight.

"Why do you separate them?" Lucia leans on the fence, wearing riding pants and a long coat of faded scarlet. Reynard touches his hat.

"The young one'll be sharpening his claws soon enough," he says. To tell the truth, he is surprised to see her, though not because she is a hero of the revolution standing in his pasture. "His mother teaches him to redirect his aggression. Not to scratch the other boys and girls."

He surveys the dale in which his paddocks sit, a flat place surrounded by hills that support thin lines of elm trees. A few storage sheds sit around the fences, and the long stable takes up one whole side of the valley. The gryphons in flight taunt the ones on the ground, then they switch places, a game that will continue all day with different players. The breeze is crisp. The whole pasture smells heavily of manure, but it is a kind, green scent Reynard has never minded.

A hinge creaks far off. From the stable, his daughter Aveline emerges, her hands soiled and her long black hair tightly restrained. Seeing Lucia, she quickens her stride toward them.

"What did you have her doing?" Lucia asks.

Reynard hardly hears: the foal has stepped back from its mother and is standing up, facing her. He's seen these youthful rebellions turn violent before. Lucia has to repeat her question before he answers, "Oh. Aveline? Nursing Dameciel's upset stomach."

"Brave woman." Lucia wrinkles her nose. "She's grown. She looks...very much like Itienne come back to us."

Reynard's thoughts stumble over an unexpected open pit. Without taking his eyes from the foal, he can tell Lucia regrets her words already, and is unaccustomed to the feeling. "Did you have something to tell me?" he asks.

"Yes." Lucia recovers herself. "I came to warn you to expect L'Escalier today. I excused myself from a meeting, in fact, in order to beat him here. I fear he'll have a proposition for you."

"On my land?" Reynard is focused first on the foal, second on how to pretend this conversation has not involved his lost wife. He is distracted, and that is a dangerous state of mind in which to deal with Sovereign Minister Dominic L'Escalier. "I don't have anywhere to receive him."

Reynard and Aveline do not live on the surface, which is for farms and gryphons. Locksgrove, the city, comes alive in the tunnels and on the cliff face. Reynard has met L'Escalier, the leader of the slave revolt, many times, but in taverns and manor offices—never here, never in his place.

"He said this could not wait."

Working every day with temperamental stallions, Reynard is well-suited to notice signs of hidden discomfort, like the clear skies that often precede storms. Lucia has taught him revolutionary scholars are not all that different from gryphons.

Something is about to happen. He waits for her to tell him what.

Lucia drops her gaze. "There's going to be a war."

So be it. Locksgrove won its last war working with far less.

But then Lucia goes on. "Not against us, you understand. Between Lascony and the Abelard League. But given that they both border us, it demands a response."

"Thank you for the warning." The foal has backed down and let the mare groom it, but Reynard swallows, wipes his brow nonetheless. "But I'm a loyal citizen. I've nothing to fear from L'Escalier."

"From whom?"

Both Reynard and Lucia startle as if caught in a tryst. Aveline, wiping her hands on a rag, smiles at their visitor.

Aveline aux Chatillon could not respect a goddess more than she does Professor Lucia Camoreux. The conscience of the revolution, a walking library at L'Escalier's side, and still gentle enough not to breathe a word of their secret meetings together. Aveline sees Lucia and Reynard standing in opposition—her skin like milky tea, his black as a gryphon's eye—and rejoices at the sudden widening of her world.

It is through knowing the Professor that she has made a decision: their pasture will do no business with Dominic L'Escalier. Sell the gryphons to farmers, to riders, to people who will care for them. Not to soldiers.

Lucia has written a book called *Treatise on the Failure of Revolutions* that Aveline is making her way through one sentence at a time. Both women hope the new Senate will take it as scripture. Previous idealistic upheavals have gone sour because their leaders became seduced into too many evils they believed were necessities. Lucia has taught Aveline that L'Escalier, without sound advice, is a prime candidate for such seduction.

Though Aveline agrees, she admits to herself that her motives are more basic: she fears for the safety of her gryphons. Last year, when Dameciel injured his wing on a windmill, she slept in the stable beside him, unable to leave for fear the infection would spread. She saw the torn, blood-spattered skin whenever she closed her eyes.

Aveline is no general. No waster of life.

Her father will object to her decision, of course. There never was a more loyal soldier of the revolution: Reynard tended mounts for L'Escalier when the revolt was still confined to back alleys and outskirt farms. But Aveline believes the best way to celebrate freedom is to exercise it occasionally.

Dominic L'Escalier wields power like a fiddler wields his bow, but her family won a war so they wouldn't have to be anybody's slaves. That goes for gryphons just as well as humans.

When Lucia tells her who is coming, Aveline gives only a tight nod. Her father does not notice anyway: he's watching his foal again before Aveline can get a sentence out.

Lucia smiles, asks if Aveline has managed to get out to see friends lately, but it has the ring of distraction. At the sound of cart wheels rolling up the dirt track, they both break off. And at the sound of a roar coming from the pasture, even her father looks up.

The roar freezes Reynard to his core. The herd is not at rest. They circle, like lightning in storm clouds.

Ouragan. Of the three stallions, this is the only one Reynard could never acclimate to the side pasture. When a creature can fly, it becomes far more dangerous for it not to know its place.

Dominic L'Escalier is standing at the outer fence, chatting with his bodyguards. Ouragan is circling, leaping to the air then strutting over the ground, around an arc that centers on the Sovereign Minister.

"Get back," Reynard tells Aveline. "Behind the shed."

"Father—"

"If I need you, I'll call! *Go!*"

Ouragan is sire to the foal birthed that morning. He's picked fights before. Foudre, never the strongest male, bears a strip of discolored fur from where Ouragan slashed his haunch with a hatchet-sized foreclaw.

Ouragan tightens his circle around the fence, bellowing and shaking his mane. Three gryphons take flight all at once, all skittish yearlings. They wheel in the air as others follow them up, an ever-widening helix of dark shapes against the clouds.

Reynard throws the side gate open and strides into the pasture as it swings shut behind him. Man and beast are alone now, enclosed together.

Ouragan veers to meet him. Reynard keeps his eyes downcast, his movements slight. Fortunately, it is overcast, so there is no danger of a shadow spooking the gryphon.

"Reynard," calls Dominic L'Escalier. His voice is cautious, and a little excited.

A roar hits Reynard's ears.

He rolls across the pasture grass. Hooves thunder by him. A wing-tip feather grazes his face, tickling.

Ouragan is charging the fence again. L'Escalier's towering guards close ranks in front of him, but they needn't bother—the stallion halts once more to face Reynard as he rises. Under the rage is a bond of trust Reynard can use. He foaled this beast, after all.

He makes it to his knees. Then he points down the road, points hard, so L'Escalier can see. To speak a warning would be too much loud noise, too fast.

The Sovereign Minister of Locksgrove swivels his head to look where Reynard is pointing. Reynard resists the urge to slap his own forehead. L'Escalier is only brilliant in two or three ways.

Ouragan snarls. His mouth froths. Reynard points to L'Escalier, then again down the road, as softly as he can, as hard as he must. At last the Minister gets it. He draws his guards by the shoulder down the road and out of sight.

"Right then," Reynard says, and smiles at Ouragan. "Now you and I can talk."

His smile is calculated. After smiling he yawns, as though he is at tea, and not much interested in it. Boredom will put the gryphon at ease.

Time to move in. Sifting his feet through the grass, his loose shirt stained with dew, Reynard approaches the wild-eyed stallion.

Ouragan roars. Reynard stands firm, though ancient instinct screams at him to run. A sudden movement now, too close to dodge, would mean death.

Two more steps. One. Arms-length away, Reynard stretches out his hand to Ouragan's mane, stroking with his fingertips. Grooming.

A new roar dies in the gryphon's throat. He pants. Reynard feels the hot breath. On the far side of the pasture, a few of the circling colts gain the courage to land.

Reynard's hands shake as he places them on either side of Ouragan's mane. His father showed him this—had his father trembled as much? *Fool,* he thinks, *the hard part is past. Now it's all rhythm.*

He breathes, in and out, seeking the pulse of Ouragan's life. Their breaths synchronize.

Ouragan looks down.

His throat rumbles, but he steps forward to nuzzle Reynard. Reynard, at the same time, looks up. Lucia stands just outside the fence, while Aveline has crept into the pasture, wielding the stout sharpened pole Reynard keeps behind the shed. Their last resort.

"Aveline," he croaks, "go and tell L'Escalier he may approach."

"Brilliant. Absolutely marvelous." L'Escalier cannot stop gushing as Reynard and Aveline lead him around the edge of the paddock. "I couldn't take my eyes off you, Reynard. At least until you ordered me to."

Reynard is glad Dominic L'Escalier has not yet asked why his mere presence frightens gryphons. He probably doesn't care. Lucia once confided in Reynard that the Minister cultivates unfamiliarity as a habit, to divert his enemies. The unfamiliar disconcerts animals.

"Every time I visit, you end up giving me orders." L'Escalier grins. "The other breeders all bow and scrape before me. Which is why I'm here."

Aveline catches her father's eye with a firm message he cannot read. She is still carrying the pike as she leads the group of six—herself, Reynard, Lucia, L'Escalier, and the two bodyguards. Inside the fence the gryphons have settled, and now the only thing in the sky is the sun, promising a radiant summer evening.

They take the Sovereign Minister all around the pasture, Reynard showing him how the operation is getting on. L'Escalier nods at all the right times, sometimes conferring with Lucia on things she seems to have mentioned to him before—"Is that the famous Foudre?" or "You were right, that shed looks fit to blow away." He is taken with the new foal, who is sharpening his claws with the enthusiasm of all nature's new children.

"Capital," he says. "Dear Reynard, if you'd accompany me back to my transport, I have a request I hope you'll consider."

Aveline is gripping the pike hard enough to snap it. She follows without being asked.

At the cart—pulled by a small mammoth of the type never allowed outside the city—L'Escalier motions his two bodyguards aboard with the driver, then turns back to the group.

"How many adults do you own, Reynard?" he asks.

"Twenty-six," Reynard says. "Three stallions, nine geldings, fourteen mares."

L'Escalier nods. He is a slight man, his nose pointed, eyes set like cut jewels into his face. "Those three will need gelding as well, then."

Aveline plants the tip of the pike in the ground. "Why?"

Her question distracts the Minister from watching the sky. "I'm sorry?"

"Why do you want to geld our stallions?" Aveline repeats.

"Sir," Reynard says.

L'Escalier waves it off. But in the split second beforehand, Reynard sees something raw and hot flood his daughter's features.

"It's the fashion in the cities of Lascony now to ride geldings in battle," L'Escalier says. "Young noble twats want to lead armies, but can't be bothered to learn enough airmanship to mount a stallion. The gelding gryphon is," he searched for a word, "predigested. But they've asked for fifty. Twenty-six is closer than twenty-three. And nobody else's will do. Not for the kind of war we're going to have."

The mammoth grunts as Lucia joins L'Escalier by the cart. Reynard suddenly understands the nature of the meeting she cut short to come warn him. "Does this mean Locksgrove has formed an alliance with Lascony?" she asks.

L'Escalier picks up the fighting note in her words and lays a hand on her shoulder. "Not an alliance, Lucia. A temporary partnership. Of mutual benefit."

"And if their enemies turn their aggression on us?"

"Lucia, my butterfly, we will talk about this later." L'Escalier clambers up into the cart, and avoids looking at Lucia's face, where a withering glare is communicating that they will talk about it at length later. "Reynard, do you accept my proposal?"

"I..." Reynard has just found his voice. "Could you repeat it, sir?"

Standing upright in the cart, L'Escalier says, "I am offering you whatever price you care to name for all twenty-six of your adult gryphons to use as war mounts for the commanders of the forces of Lascony to use in their swift conquest of their opponents, the Abelard League, who are now are mutual enemies. Do you accept?"

"Father," Aveline hisses, as Lucia refuses L'Escalier's hand and mounts the cart alone, "that's our entire breeding stock."

Does she think I don't know? No matter how many he sells to private buyers, simply knowing Lucia reminds Reynard daily that a fledgling nation of former slaves cannot afford luxuries like unfettered commerce. He sought out Dominic L'Escalier's cause in his life's one moment of white-hot rage, watched the one-time manor slave drill barely-armed troops and quote philosophers in his speeches, and has known ever since: the Minister is the father of freedom. There can be no repaying a debt to him.

And war? asks Aveline in his head. *Is war not a luxury?*

It is not a choice. They have never been his gryphons. They have always been Locksgrove's. L'Escalier's.

Aveline shouts, "Never," as Reynard says, "Yes."

The upper tunnels, unlike the tide-washed slums at the cliff base, are clean, and well lit by skylights that allow shrubs to grow. Other than the mammoth traffic, this neighborhood—reserved by L'Escalier for government employees—is quiet.

Smoke from a fire, scented with cinnamon, drifts along the tunnel, wide enough for three mammoths abreast. The beasts prefer it down here, out of the sun, where their shaggy coats don't make them sweat.

Aveline skirts around one. She's been keeping ahead of Reynard all the way home. She pushes through a red curtain into their main chamber without holding it open. Reynard walks into it.

No matter how many times L'Escalier offers him a palace on the cliff face, Reynard doesn't want to move. He and Aveline each have their own room, and the kitchen is in a third, all separated from the main chamber by their own curtains. Aveline is brushing hers aside when Reynard enters.

He calls her name. She sighs and turns around. The large dining table sits between them.

"Will you explain why you disrespected me in front of Dominic and Lucia this afternoon?"

"You know damn well why, father. What were you thinking? Every last stallion and mare sold off for Lascon nobles to prance around on?"

"Watch your tongue." He moves around the table; she keeps her distance. "We have the colts and the yearlings, and it's still the foaling season. I won't sell a pregnant mare. We'll get new breeding stock."

"I don't care about the breeding stock!" she snaps. "Did you raise Ouragan and

Foudre and the others to fight wars? They'll die on the ends of pikes!"

A heavy hand clutches Reynard's stomach. She does indeed look a great deal like her mother.

"The gryphons aren't ours," he says. "We raise them for those who will buy them. We must sell outside Locksgrove if that's where the market is."

"Amazing." Aveline's words are made of ice. "L'Escalier is back at the palace, but I can still hear him talking. Tell me, father, what do you call a living being that can be bought and sold at its owner's whim?"

"I call it my job!" At some point Reynard begins to shout. "I do what I was born for. What others do with it is not my concern."

"Then I was wrong. It's not just the gryphons enslaved. It's you."

It is as though she has slugged him in the gut. The wind whistles out of his lungs and he collapses into a hardwood chair. Aveline looks more appalled than angry— she may not have meant to say so much— but her features harden again. She disappears behind her bedroom curtain, and returns carrying a wax tablet, which she thrusts at Reynard.

Handwriting runs across it in several rows. Of course, Reynard cannot understand it, but he can tell every other row was written by a practiced hand. Every second row is scratched more messily, though the writing tightens by the end.

He recognizes the script of the odd-numbered rows. He has seen it on letters from the university, the ones he glances at before going in search of someone to read them to him.

"Lucia's been giving me lessons," Aveline says. "I'm learning to read and write. I won't spend my life tending war machines, father. I won't be a slave."

Reynard struggles to stand. He lays the tablet on the chair so he doesn't drop it. "You're turning your back on everything we are."

"You turned first. What about mother? What would she say about this war?"

This is enough. So Aveline wants to hurt him. Very well. He is a strong man. He can hurt back.

"You don't know what you're talking about," he hisses. "You weren't five years old when the chains broke. You know nothing of slavery. And less of your mother."

"Then tell me." Aveline stands her ground. "Tell me all about how beautiful she was. She must have had a lustrous mane, and silky wings. You've never cared for anything without wings."

When Reynard gathers himself after this, he is sitting in one of the hardwood chairs, warmed by a fire he doesn't recall starting. Aveline must be in her room, or out on the streets looking for one of her friends. He makes a pot of stew with fresh vegetables and broth, leaves a bowl out as a peace offering. It grows cold.

Long after the skylight darkens, he notices he sat on the wax tablet with the writing lesson. He hauls himself up, joints snapping, to put it someplace out of the way.

The foaling season passes. Aveline refuses to have anything to do with the adult gryphons, spends all her time exercising and grooming the yearlings. She cleans the stable, then cleans it again, and does everything she can to avoid her father. Once, she respected his willful determination to soldier forth on his own course no matter the consequences; now her old respect sickens her.

When the appointed day comes, the mares and geldings are led through the paddock gates into waiting trailers whose cloth coverings are emblazoned with the blue boar of Lascony. Each gryphon folds its wings and munches at the oats left for it, while the Lascon drivers lock the rear gate. Even Ouragan goes quietly, though Reynard has to lead him in by hand.

The trailers take them to the front lines, to the scraps of land Lascony and the Abelard League have been struggling over for longer than Reynard or L'Escalier have been alive. The gryphons fly over these provinces, bearing commanders who urge soldiers forward. The Lascons later use them as scouts. When things go bad, they become bombers.

They are struck with arrows, rocks from slings, ballista bolts. Many gryphons together can turn the tide of a battle, but the more who appear in the same sky, the more seem to die.

One day at the beginning of autumn, more than half the remaining gryphons cross a churning river to plant a bridge for the Lascon army to cross. A hidden Abelard ambush force surges out of the underbrush before the Lascons can hammer the planks into place. They throw nets at the gryphons and stab them and their riders with pitchforks until long after they die. Trapped on the other side of the river, the other Lascons are crushed by the main Abelard force. Less than half escape. Ouragan, the fierce, throws his untrained rider and takes to the sky, but a crossbow fusillade shreds his wing and sends him crashing to the ground. He dies on impact, a last act of rebellion against the men awaiting the satisfaction of butchering him with scimitars.

Two days after, the news reaches Locksgrove. Dominic L'Escalier walks out of a senate meeting, in the middle of a speech, and sends his steward to find Reynard aux Chatillon. Once again, Lucia arrives first, and finds Aveline, who, seeing the Professor hastily wiping mucus and tears from her face, knows instantly what has been lost.

Reynard descends into a café on the cliff face, on the fifth level of a boardwalk that rises another six stories above their heads. Tables form a constellation on the wooden walkway before the shop, which is recessed into the stone. L'Escalier has already claimed a table, and ordered two overlarge mugs of coffee. The other tables are empty.

L'Escalier gets up to pull out Reynard's chair. "I hope you don't mind the short notice," he says, "or the venue. This place used to be a big-time exporter's private roaster. His old house slave runs it now."

"What is it you want?" Reynard asks, rubbing his eyes. The coffee smells dark and strong.

"We can't just talk?" L'Escalier takes a long sip. "I'd have met you somewhere with stronger spirits, but it's hardly noon, and I need to keep a bit of respect with the people."

Reynard stifles a yawn. Aveline still does her share of the work in the pasture —more, if anything—but speaks to him two and three words at a time, and not at all when the work is done. Since their fight, he has not slept well.

L'Escalier sighs. "Very well. Yes. I do need your help."

Some giggling from below, maybe the crowd around a street performer. Someone wheels a cart along the next boardwalk up.

L'Escalier asks, "Have you heard the news from the war?"

Reynard feels a chill. He wishes he were back with the colts. "Nothing to do with me. Sir."

"Impressive that you should have missed it. I can't get people to talk about anything else." L'Escalier forces on a smile. Reynard gulps the bitter coffee. "The truth is it might have more to do with you than you realize. You helped Lascony once. They—or I—we're hoping you might do it again."

So that's what this is. Reynard's eyes drift out to sea. The sky is steel-grey, the breakers on the ocean like cold white fingers. Autumn is roaring past.

He hears himself say, "I can't. I only have colts and yearlings, not ready to ride. Find someone else."

L'Escalier shakes his head, lowers his voice. "There's no-one else. The others breed work animals or poncy show mares for rich traders. We are a new city, Reynard, without many options. You have the only war mounts I trust."

Dominic L'Escalier alienated Reynard's daughter, enslaved the things he cared most about, to die in a war about which they understood even less than he does. Now the Minister wants to do it again. To gryphons even less prepared, who will die even faster.

He could not have done any of these things had Reynard not consented. By the breaking of his chains, Reynard himself has been broken.

Reynard stands up and kicks the chair back, knocking it into another. "Tell Lascony you're done. I'm not selling the colts. They can't carry the payloads you want and they'll spook at crossbow fire."

"Sit down," L'Escalier says. "Drink your coffee until you can think rationally. Remember we have an agreement."

"We had a—" Reynard fumbles for words. "A business relationship. I don't work for you."

Now L'Escalier is standing as well, his mug forgotten. "You work for your city. Do you understand what's going on out there? The Abelards are marching on the Lascon capital. If they take it, and that is a matter of weeks," he pounds his knuckles on the table, rattling the mugs, "they will make Lascony a client state. And there is *nothing* between Lascony and Locksgrove save the few thousand militiamen the Senate can draft. We'll be overrun."

He steps around the table, looking up a bit to stare into Reynard's eyes. "Ask Lucia. She can read the signs, Reynard. Do you want to wear chains again? Do you want to go back to being a slave?"

Reynard lurches forward. L'Escalier narrows his eyes. "Go ahead. I didn't bring a bodyguard. Watch. *I order you to come out, guards!*"

Neither of his usual hulks materializes. The proprietor of the shop is stock-still with his hands in a vat of soapy water.

"Strike me," L'Escalier says. "But then say yes. Do you want them to take your daughter, Reynard? Do you know what they do to pretty girls like Aveline when they sack cities? Are your yearlings worth more to you than keeping her from that fate?"

Reynard's fist connects with L'Escalier's jaw. The Minister stumbles. He catches himself on the edge of another table and turns back to Reynard.

"Do it again, if you must."

Reynard digs his nails into his palm, and turns, caring only to put distance between himself and this man who burns everything he touches.

"Air support, Reynard," L'Escalier calls after him. "Scouting. Leadership. Flanking maneuvers. Evacuating the wounded. The Abelards dispatched entire cohorts against your gryphons. They determined the course of battles."

He stops. Without turning, he says, "I didn't raise them for that."

"Why did you raise them?"

A fisherman is rowing through the bay, headed for home. There is about to be rain. The eyes of the silent, waiting Minister drive Reynard into his own head, toward a fight with this question he has never before dared to meet.

"For the same reason you hold power and start wars," he tells L'Escalier. "Because we are good at nothing else."

"I didn't start this war." L'Escalier steps close again and whispers. "The Abelards despise us, Reynard. They wish we did not exist. Lascony alone keeps their wish from coming true, and there's about to be no more Lascony, unless you let go of your moon-damned yearlings."

Clear as day, Reynard sees each of the gryphons he has raised since he inherited the paddock. Unfolding its wings for the first time. Scratching at grass and bark and the walls of the paddock while its mother guided it around. Taking flight for the first time, its roars joyful, like a human child running for the sake of running. Its muscles flowing like water, with no motion wasted. Carrying a commander out to the battlefield. Falling from the sky, punctured with pikes, life leaking out.

Cursing Reynard aux Chatillon, with their last breaths, for delivering them life only to send them back into slavery to save his own skin from the same fate. Condemning him, in some strange gryphon language he would never speak, for his crime of delivering a human daughter into the praxis of suffering.

He cannot unburden himself of his debt. Cannot decide for a whole city. Nor for Aveline.

He says, "Yes."

Aveline and Lucia leave the University campus at dusk. It is hard to tell the time, since few people in the low tunnels are bothering to maintain the light cycles anymore. They stay huddled in their caverns with their families, or flee to sea, crowding the bay with boats. Collisions have occurred. Aveline doesn't know where they think they're going.

She herself is going to the empty pasture to take Lucia to shelter with Reynard—though she isn't certain Reynard knows why people are hiding. During their lesson, Aveline had to tell Lucia how her father sits in the shack most days, staring at the wall. They still are not talking, but she has begun to bring her father tea, which he sometimes even drinks.

Lucia can explain to him that the fall of Lascony took three days, and that Dominic L'Escalier has fled the city. None of it shocked Aveline, but to tell Reynard his one-time hero has abandoned Locksgrove will require Lucia's gentler touch. Her father still wants desperately to believe the Sovereign Minister is good.

A left, and a right. A few tunnels remain, and then they will be at the pasture. They're close enough to the surface to tell it's raining. *Will they drag us all away from here?* she thinks. *Will all these tunnels will start leaking, with nobody to maintain the seals? Will the gryphons that are left go feral? Will they prefer it that way? Will they remember us?*

In the shack, with wind howling and rain dripping through the roof, Aveline asks Reynard and Lucia about slavery.

Reynard is stuffing plaster into the cracks in the shed, blotting out a rain-washed view of the pasture with each one he closes. He wants to keep doing this for a while. There are some holes left. But then Aveline asks again in a small voice —"What is it going to be like?"—and Lucia can't answer.

His daughter needs him. It is the first time in a long time. Even before she turned against him, they were more like business partners than anything else.

Lucia is sitting on a sack of oats. She has unbuckled and unsheathed a long, gently-curved sword, and placed it on the table. Aveline is on the floor in the corner, her knees drawn up around her long pike. Reynard drops into one of the chairs.

"Not a death sentence," he says. "Some people made a good life. My father did, and his father. If you have a trade, you become more...more valuable."

"Reynard," Lucia says, but Aveline interrupts her. "I want the truth. All of it. Did slavery kill Mom?"

Lucia closes her eyes, rests her hand on the sword hilt. Reynard's throat clenches. He nods. "Your mother died because she was a slave."

The wind howls through the following silence. Amid the drumming of rain and the scent of wet wood, Reynard realizes they expect him to explain how she died. He will do it to fill the silence.

"The revolution didn't happen overnight. Much as it looked like it did." A gust of wind reaches into the lantern on the middle of the table, flickering the flame. "There were other fights. Earlier. In the streets, in the pastures, field slaves against the house. Itienne, your mother... she was out too late. Some people had died the night before."

"Slave or free?" Aveline asks.

"Don't remember." Reynard is talking now the way he breathed long ago with wild dead Ouragan. With the memory they enter the same rhythm, drawing strength from each other. With the story they survive a bit longer. "She walked into the middle of a skirmish. Not far from here. Carrying eggs. Our mistress wanted some."

He swallows. "Both sides said they don't know who hit her. And I never found out. I buried her the same night."

Now everyone falls quiet. Lucia grips the sword hilt. Reynard squeezes the wall putty in his hands, then, all of a sudden, drops it.

Aveline perks up. "Did you hear—"

"Voices." Lucia takes up the sword. "Both of you stay here."

Aveline jumps to her feet with the pike. "I'm coming with you."

Reynard finds the strength to stand. "You are not."

There's a pitchfork in a hay pile, ten paces away from the door. If he can reach it and return before any Abelard soldiers appear, he and Lucia might be able to bottleneck them in the shed door.

He doesn't know when he decided to fight, or to die. Perhaps it was the story, but more likely it was Aveline, who now gives him a look in response to his injunction. It is defiant, nakedly so, but not contemptuous. She does not mean to hurt him. She is like the wax tablet now, a simple statement of fact, telling him the way things are.

And it's all right. Just because she can protect herself, doesn't mean he can't protect her too.

Lucia puts her hand on the door. "If they have lights, we can sneak up on them. If not, nobody leaves this room."

"I need to run for the pitchfork," Reynard says. "They'll have armor. I can't fight bare-handed."

Lucia recalculates in her mind. The voice comes again, and Reynard strains to listen, but he can't pick any one out of the wind.

"All right. They may well still be too far away to see us in the dark. When I open the door, run to the hay pile. Then keep quiet and surprise them from behind."

Reynard nods. There isn't time for anything else. Lucia grips the edge of the door. Throws it open.

He runs. The ground vanishes under his feet. The paddock is dark, but the Abelards are carrying a light that shines a demonic red over the fences and pasture. Reynard grabs the pitchfork out of the hay pile, and whirls around.

Somebody shouts from within the paddock. "Lucia! Reynard!"

Reynard freezes. An Abelard might know Lucia's name. Maybe. But his?

"Lucia! Aveline! *Reynard!*"

He hears a sword strike point-first into soil, then, right after, a fist hitting bone. Rushing with the pitchfork, he arrives in the pool of light at the same time as

Aveline, who lodges her pike in the tines of his weapon so he cannot move it.

Reynard turns from her to the man lying on the ground, who's managed to hold onto the torch despite Lucia having knocked him flat. Just one of Dominic L'Escalier's many talents.

"I deserved that," he admits. "But please don't do it again."

"Why not?" In the half-light, the sword glows like the blade of some ancient hero. Reynard and Aveline enter the paddock, where Dominic is getting to his feet under the watchful and enraged eyes of Lucia. "Tell me why."

Dominic holds out his hands. Other than the torch, he's unarmed. "You want to know what I did."

"I know what you did. Ran off in the night and struck a bargain with the Abelards. How many of us did you sell? Thirty percent? Fifty?"

"You're right." He dodges another blow, quickly adding, "Half-right. I did strike a deal, but I didn't sell humans. Don't you see?" He looks straight at Reynard. "I sold gryphons."

Reynard had thought this was done hurting him. But there is more still. "What do you mean?" he asks.

Dominic straightens up. "I already told you what a difference they make on the battlefield. Two dozen of them can be worth a whole light infantry, if a good general knows how to use them. They're living weapons."

Reynard is thinking of the foals in first flight, of the power of their wingbeats as he loses them in the sunrise. There is no creature in the world that knows so well where it's going.

"The Abelard League has wanted their own mounted force since they first fought the Lascon gryphons. And they were prepared to take Locksgrove to do it—their country is all mountains and mines, no pastureland. But they didn't want to. I mean, look at you three. Look at us. Everyone in this city is armed. Maybe the revolutionary militia can't stand up to a trained fighting force, but they would have had to fight tunnel by tunnel through the underground, with clubs and pikes hiding in every cavern." Dominic straightens up. "They'd have won. But with heavy losses. Nobody is ever going to take this city without watering the caves with blood. It's the way we're built."

"So you offered an alternative," Lucia says. "Trade money for the breeding stock, instead of lives."

"I told them we could only sell colts and yearlings, but they were happier with that than with losing them to the enemy."

"So war can go on in peace," Aveline mutters. "Having gained a third dimension."

Dominic turns toward Reynard. "I'm sorry I didn't tell you, but to be honest, I didn't think of the plan until yesterday. There wasn't time to explain."

"So it's over," Lucia says. "We're arms dealers to the continent now."

"You must admit it's a fine role to play," Dominic replies. "Everyone needs us alive and selling more than they need us destroyed."

"Yes," Lucia says, taking up the sword and sheathing it. Her eyes are dark, and when Dominic reaches out a hand to her, she neither takes it nor responds at all. "Yes. I must admit that."

Reynard drops the pitchfork with a thud. While Dominic is distracted, he takes the torch out of the Minister's hand, then turns.

Dominic jerks around. "Reynard—"

Behind him, though he doesn't see, Lucia throws her arm out. "Let him have the light. He'll need it."

"But where's he going?"

"I don't know. And don't ask. He's the one you made pay, Dominic. Not the Abelard League."

Another weapon hits the dirt. Someone hurtles toward the shed. Reynard keeps walking.

Once the tunnel city of Locksgrove is no longer underfoot, the pastureland turns to forest. The woods drip year-round with mist, the needles on the trees heavy with water, the soil slick with mud. There are just three roads. On one of these, Dominic met with the Abelard ambassadors. On the day the revolution began, fog made solid walls over all three.

Aveline follows her father's torch to the edge of the woods before she musters the will to call out to him. These trees have a threshold: the last farms clear-cut such a perfect line one can stand with a foot in and a foot out of the forest.

"Father."

He turns. It is light enough to see his face.

"Did you know I was following you?"

"I didn't," Reynard admits. "I knew I wanted to walk. Not much else."

"Why here?" She is drawing nearer. In addition to her pike—more of a walking stick now—and her coat, she has brought several yards of rope. "You're not a woodsman."

"No. But your great-grandfather was. Did I ever tell you?"

He must have looked like you, she thinks.

"He captured the ancestors of all the gryphons we sold," Reynard says. "Day by day, in the woods, never able to get farther than the line of soldiers stationed on the other side to capture fugitives. In two years, he brought back twenty-six. That's been a good number for our family."

"I brought this." Aveline drops the bundle of rope at her feet. "To make snares. Or a net."

He stares at her. His surprise, Aveline thinks, must mirror her own. Didn't she hate this man? Didn't she rail every day against his weak will, his blind equation of L'Escalier to the whole city? Hadn't he made war on the Abelards?

No, she thinks. *No. He didn't.*

Reynard takes the coil of rope in his hand.

"Get new breeding stock," Aveline tells him. "And keep breeding. Father, you're the best at it. L'Escalier knows, everyone knows. So rebuild the pasture. No more staring at the wall." She points at the woods with her pike. "Get in there."

"Why?" her father asks. "Aveline...you were ready to abandon all of this."

She shakes her head, dries her eyes. "I didn't understand what Lucia was trying to teach me. Or to teach all of us. Nothing is good on its own. Sometimes, we just face down charging stallions, and...right at those moments the only thing that makes sense is to be kind."

Aveline lays her hands on her father's shoulders. "We can make them good, father. They're not weapons or even tools, they're hopes, yours and mine and their own. We can raise the gryphons free."

There is a long silence, broken by morning birdsong from within the trees. At last, Reynard says, "I think so too."

Aveline backs off, suddenly confused. "You do? And you came here without any equipment? What were you going to do, wrestle them?"

"I suppose..." These words are not calculated. She perceives he has just thought of them. "I suppose I was waiting for you to bring the rope."

In the next moment, a moment that lasts a long time, Aveline is grateful for the knowledge she has taken for herself. Not everyone knows the instant they have made a decision that will alter the rest of their life, but she does now. She will follow her father into the forest, into his understanding of beautiful doomed things. She will accept his skills, but she will also read and write, and in doing so, perhaps will save Locksgrove by saving the creatures it has made.

The best of it. The best of her father.

"Come on," Reynard says. "It's just early enough to catch one still asleep."

He slings the rope across his shoulders, and they step together into the shadows.

About the story

I came up with the world of Locksgrove during a worldbuilding exercise with friends. It's based on revolutionary Haiti, with Dominic L'Escalier a stand-in for Toussaint L'Overture. Reynard aux Chatillon was a later addition, partially based on Jiro Horikoshi, the Japanese aircraft engineer whose dilemma is chronicled in Hayao Miyazaki's film *The Wind Rises*.

Reynard and Jiro share the same central dilemma, one also faced by Albert Einstein--if you're brilliant at something, should you do it, regardless of the consequences? In addition to this, I wanted to use the meeting of history and fantasy to discuss questions of slavery, freedom, and politics. Does a nation have a morality? If so, what responsibilities do the people in it hold?

After Haiti successfully established the only nation of revolutionary former slaves, Thomas Jefferson, among others, advocated for an international boycott of

Haitian trade--in order to discourage other oppressed populations from following in Haiti's path. For all his high rhetoric about the Tree of Liberty, Jefferson's loyalty was to the economy in the end.

At the opening of "The Foaling Season," Locksgrove is in a similar predicament. At the heart of it is the question of what the gryphons mean: they could be symbols, pets, companions, or dumb products to be merchandised out. L'Escalier doesn't believe Reynard has the luxury to think of them as anything but the latter. Reynard's daughter Aveline feels differently.

In the end, though, I knew that I wanted the story to affirm the status of the gryphons as actors with their own agency.

A question for the author

Q: What is your favourite short story?

A: "Night Meeting" by Ray Bradbury from The Martian Chronicles. Nothing much happens in it--just a guy driving to a party and meeting a Martian on the way. During their conversation, however, Earthling and Martian realize they cannot tell the difference between future and past, and that therefore the only thing we can count on is the beauty of the present. Bradbury uses simple images to immensely moving effect. The whole book is great, but this is the one I can read over and over.

Honorable mentions: "Seasons of Glass and Iron" by Amal El-Mohtar, "Idle Days on the Yann" by Lord Dunsany, "Oh, Whistle, and I'll Come to You, My Lad" by M.R. James.

About the author

Samuel Chapman was born in Minnesota and raised in Wales. He lives in Walla Walla, WA, where he writes novels and short stories, fences at a classical salle, and works in water rights. In past jobs he's been a land steward, tour guide, writing tutor, bookstore clerk, and crew on a tall ship.

www.samuelpchapman.wordpress.com, @samuelchapman93

Nobody's Daughters and the Tree of Life

L'Erin Ogle

The sun is just bellying up above the skyline and light filters through the world. I turn Star away from the Deadlands, where there aren't any trees or shrubs and the sun has scorched the ground into big puzzle pieces. A long time ago, there used to be fertile land here, like our farm a mile down the road, but Nobody happened and now nothing grows.

Nobody's story is sort of like The Nightmare Man, or the Hissing Man, things that come from Before, back when there was magic all around. The Nightmare Man has long octopus arms with suction cup mouths that let him climb houses in the dark to steal children. The Hissing Man comes while you're sleeping and hisses little snakes in your ear that slither around your brain. Nobody was a witch who cursed the Old town when she was murdered. They say there's a tree of life that grew right from her body, but I figure they call it the Deadlands for a reason.

But the stories, they're not real, you know. The dolls in our living room, they're the ones who scare me, lined up with their flat dead glass eyes.

They're my momma's dolls. She started buying them after she lost the first baby, back when I was a baby myself. They come from a special maker, clear out east of the main cities. She's got fourteen at last count, all fair skinned and with long sleek hair that she brushes and braids. Momma has lost all the babies since me. They come half formed, months too early. They don't look nothing like babies. We bury the tiny bodies out at the far end of the orchards. Afterwards, Momma lies in bed with eyes just as flat and lifeless as the dolls.

It's awful hard on her. She wants a girl something fierce. When she forgets all the sad things, she comes out to watch me ride Star. When she was my age, she used to race all the other kids on her horse. She won every time. She had long hair that ran out behind her like a banner. Then her sister Juliet tried to race with her and the big kids, went off her horse, got trampled. Momma was responsible for her, and she rode home with Juliet's body all crumpled up and torn, and then she didn't never ride again.

Today, we are almost two thirds through the baby growing. Me and Momma took a great big white square piece of paper and chalked out two hundred boxes. We made rows of ten, layers of twenty. On good days when the noises aren't banging into her eardrums and setting off the bees inside her head, she lets me make a big X through a box. Bad days, she does it all alone. Those days she doesn't come out of bed except to make the X.

Sometimes on good days, her smile comes so bright I can feel my heart bloom inside my chest.

Sweat's already thick on Star. August is scorching all of us alive this year. Even the trees have leaves browning and shriveling up at the edges. I stuck to the grassy trails on my morning ride to keep my lungs from seizing up. I saw when Grandpa and Dad rode for the bank this morning, clouds of dust spinning up from the horses' hooves in circles, lazy spinning devils.

I get home, unsaddle Star and turn him out, start chores. I start by feeding the animals. We have about thirty horses, a couple dozen chickens for laying eggs. I collect the speckled eggs, then I count all the yearlings — a dozen — and stop to watch the foals playing near their mothers, with their soft fuzzy tails and long stilt legs. Pretty soon, we'll have to separate them from their mothers. When that happens, both sets of them will cry for a couple days. The sound hurts me inside. I sit with them, the babies, as long as I can, trying to console them with tiny crab apples from the orchards, and petting them, but it just takes time.

You can get used to anything, over time.

After chores, I stay outside and lay under the trees, chewing blades of grass. I love the taste of grass. Mama complains about my teeth turning green, but I can't stop. There's nothing like a fresh blade of grass. It tastes like everything's beginning again.

"Alvie!" Momma screams, her voice uncoiling from the house down towards me.

I run up to the house, through the front door, catching it with my back foot so it doesn't bang, then past all the dolls with their wide open eyes, straight to her door. I knock soft, and she says, "Alvie, come now!"

She's sitting up in bed, her hair in dark ringlets hanging around her face. She's sweating, and it darkens the neckline of her thin gown, sticking it to her. She's got her hands down between her legs, and though it's dark, lit only by a glass lantern on the bureau, I can see dark streaks of blood on her knuckles.

"Go fetch the doctor, and hurry, boy," she says. "There's still time."

I don't mess around. Back past the dolls, out the door, stop, don't let it bang, run to the stable. Star picks his head up when I enter and I just grab the bridle and slip it on. I don't bother with the saddle, just open the stall door and stand on his water bucket to mount. Then we're out and into a trot, even though I should warm him up with a walk. I'm trying to keep from digging my heels into him, let him set the pace. Maybe if I ride fast enough, pray hard enough, the baby will live.

I've been so quiet this summer, making sure I'm not even hardly around. The problem with being quiet is that everything makes noise. Peeing, chewing food, even just rolling over in bed. Forget getting dressed and chewing. Sometimes Mama hears the noise ten times as loud and it turns into bees that buzz around her head so she can't sleep or eat. It stresses her out, sends out bad feelings.

This summer I mostly just used the house for sleeping, spent most of my time at the stables or with Grandpa, living in the house he and Grandma built, just over the hill. Grandpa and I play a lot of rummy at nights, because he won't teach me poker until I'm fourteen.

I ride for the doctor's. He's the only other person within five miles of us. I don't take the road but cut Star towards the orchards. He's not much to look at, knock-kneed and his overbite that makes him look sort of dumb, but he's sure-footed and quick and he can manage the tree roots and the trail winding up through the trees to the doctor's farm.

Star gets us there quick in spite of the heat. Theodore, the doctor, is sitting on his porch, watching me race up the drive. When I get there, he asks, "Addalynn?"

"She says the baby's coming," I say. Star's sides are heaving, and I dismount so's to lighten his load.

"Aye," he says. His hair gets more silver every year, even though he isn't that old through the face. I think he's about halfway between Momma and Grandpa's age. I've only ever ridden by before, and I sneak a peek around him to size the place up.

You can tell the mettle of a man by the way he takes care of things. That's what Grandpa says. And the doctor is always neat and clean, his horse groomed well. His house is glossy wood, and there are plants and flowers blooming everywhere. They crawl up the side of the house, curling around the shutters, explosions of bright red and violet ad yellow. The leaves span as big as my hands, with saw toothed edges and veins of blue and dark green running through them.

"Had a feeling," he says. "Why don't you saddle up my horse, Alvie. I'll gather my things."

I tack up his bay mare he rides, and a little chestnut filly watches me from her stall. She's got big liquid brown eyes, and

I wonder why I haven't seen her before. I bring the mare back around to the front of the house, stick my hand in my pocket and pull out grass to chew. My nerves are shaking, and the grass helps.

He comes out and places his saddlebags across the back, mounts up. We start down the drive together. I gesture at the trail that snakes down through the orchards.

"I took the back way here," I say, "but it's pretty uneven. Star's real sure of foot."

"Take the back way again," he says. His eyes crinkle and I think it's his version of smiling. "This mare of mine's big, but she's nimble."

When we get back, Grandpa and Dad's horses are in front of the stable. Their reins are tethered but they're still saddled, sweating in the sun. It's the hottest part of the year, and I'm surprised Grandpa left them like that. Without being asked, I reach over and take the doctor's horse's reins, tell him I'll guide the horses in and cool them down. He nods once, dismounts with his bags, and disappears inside. He stops to let the door close softly, so he knows Mama's condition.

I take the horses out and unsaddle them, lead them to the south corral, smaller than a pasture, but shady with a big water trough. I leave Star, Grandpa's horse, and the doctor's horse in the corral and take Daddy's stallion to the barn. Doesn't appear anyone's in heat, but best to be safe. Dad always rides a stallion, but Grandpa prefers mares and geldings, says they're loyal, says a stud will abandon you when his blood is up.

Grandpa comes out after a while, fitting his wide brimmed hat down and shielding his eyes. He's already got his pipe out to pack it, and he's pinching fat shreds of tobacco between his fingers. His hands are heavy with yellow calluses. He's got thick twists for knuckles, from his arthritis. He smokes all the time unless he's eating or working. Sometimes he even smokes while he works, his pipe clenched between his teeth.

He's the one who showed me how to get a skittish horse to come to me. He always smells like burning wood, and he always shows me how to do things.

"How you doing, Alvie?" he says, clapped me on the shoulder.

"Ok. How's Mama?"

"Not so good, son. Remember last year, when that little bay mare got a foal hung up in her?"

I remembered. She was laid up on her side, heaving with it, two tiny hooves hanging out of her. Grandpa had to push the foal back in that time, turn it. It took some doing, the veins in his neck says. The mare survived, but the foal didn't. Grandpa was mad at himself for it. He doesn't like losing life.

"Can't the doctor get it out?"

"He's getting it," he says. "But-well, there's a lot of damage."

The best thing about Grandpa is he's no bullshit. He says so himself. "She's going to be alright, though, right?"

"Aye," he says. "But she won't be having any babies, Alvie."

It takes a minute to sink in.

I'm thinking on it, trying to figure out if that means Mama will get better or worse, when I realize Grandpa's tapping the ashes from his pipe and grinding them out with his heel. He looks as tired as I've ever seen him.

"Need a favor, Alvie," he says.

"Aye, Grandpa."

"I need you to ride back up to Ted's house." My grandpa is the only person I ever heard call my momma Addy instead of Adalynn, or the doctor Ted instead of Theodore. "Fetch his wife Mattie."

"I didn't know he had a wife," I say.

"Aye. Ride my horse up and tell her Hans needs her help with his daughter."

"Yes, sir," I say.

He puts his heavy, wrinkled hand on my shoulder. It's warm, like always, and my muscles loosen a little. Grandpa always knows what to do.

I don't have to look for the doctor's wife. She's in the yard, a big mass of gold red hair sprouting from a knot on the top of her head. She hears me coming and stands up. She's just a tiny splinter of a woman. She's about as tall as me, slender bones and big bright eyes. She's got a shimmer about her, something shining inside. It's not anything I can put words to. It does something inside me, makes me ache. It's like a beautiful horse full out running, or a foal perching for the first time on their own legs, wobbling in the moonlight, or what it's like to kiss a girl.

"You must be Alvie," she says, song like.

"Aye, ma'am."

"Mattie," she says. She brushes her hands on her pants and comes towards me with her hand reaching out.

I lean down and shake it, after rubbing my own sweaty hand on my leg.

"Is everything all right?" she asks.

"My grandpa says to ask you to come help," I say. I squint to see her better, but she's all wrapped up in shimmering light.

"Aye," she says. "Well, then. Would you mind getting my horse for me?"

"Aye," I say, and dismount, tethering Grandpa's mare to the little post by the porch. I fetch the chestnut filly and get her ready. Bring her around and Mattie's ready, different pants, hair wound into a braid that creeps over her shoulder and down her side.

We start back towards home.

"I'm sorry to hear about your momma," she says. "Are you all right, Alvie?"

"It's Momma who's sick," I say. "Not me."

"Yes, but it can't be easy for you, either," she says.

I don't say nothing, just put my head down.

She hums for a minute. "Ted and I don't have any children, you know."

"Why?" I ask. I know she wants me to.

"Some sort of incompatibility," she says. She shrugs. "Not meant to be. Most people would only think about how hard it is on me, but it's hard on Ted, too. Just like this must be hard on you."

My stomach twists up in a knot. I take out more grass, start to chew it. "I'm all right," I say. "I just hope maybe this time she's far enough along. I prayed every night, since I knew."

"Aye," she says. "To the old gods?"

"Aye."

She doesn't say anything else. We get home and find Grandpa and Dad stone still on the porch, waiting. We ride right up to them, and Mattie asks what the word is.

"Ted says she'll be all right, but he's got more bleeding to control," Grandpa says.

Dad wasn't looking anywhere but at Mattie, who kept silent. "What's this, now?"

"Send Ted out," Grandpa says, and Dad goes like he always does when Grandpa tells him something.

The doctor comes straight out. "What the hell's this, Mattie?"

Mattie slides from her horse, dropping the reins to the ground, and goes right up to him. "Easy, Ted," she says. She rests her hands on his waist, her cheek against his chest. He puts an arm around her but his eyes, dark and narrow behind his lenses, never move from Grandpa's.

"Aye," Grandpa says, but that was all.

Something's twisted up between the three of them, that I can see sharp edges on but can't make out the shape.

"No," the doctor says, but he says it to Mattie this time. He drops his chin on the top of her head. They go together so easy I can't tell where one ends and the other begins.

"Addy's my only child, Ted," Grandpa says. "I aim to get her a baby girl. She won't quit trying until she's dead."

"She's got a handsome son, and hell with that damned tree," the doctor says. "She won't let you take a baby from it without taking her own pound of flesh." The color's gone from his lips but rising his cheeks.

"Aye," Grandpa says. "I understand there's a price to pay."

"Then go by yourself, you damn fool."

"I have to go," she says, and she catches his eyes again for a long moment, and I see his answer in the way he looks back at her, like she's the entire universe.

"I'm Nobody's daughter, Ted. Maybe that means something."

"Mattie, it won't matter."

"Ted," she says. "I love you, but I owe Hans and your mother my whole life."

Ted's lips get even thinner, scar tissue white against his teeth. "If anything happens to her—"

"On my life, nothing will," Grandpa says. "You have my word."

Grandpa leaves them, goes to fill his canteen. I follow behind him, so close I step on his heels. "Where are you going? What tree?"

"Nobody's tree. The baby tree," he says, short.

"What's that?"

"You know about Nobody, everyone knows that story," he says.

Nobody was a girl stuck between worlds, who stumbled out of a pond one day in front of a bunch of kids. She couldn't speak, and no one knew what to do with her, but a girl took her home to her family. They tried to make her normal, but Nobody couldn't be normal. She had something inside her, maybe like the doctor's wife, that made people go sort of nuts. One day, she got tired of our world and tried to go back home, through the pond, but whatever door she had come through, was gone. When she climbed out of the pond, some boys had followed her. No one that tells the story will say exactly what happened after, but Nobody died. The boys didn't want to get caught so they cut her body open and filled it with stones from the shore. She sank to the bottom, and all the fish died. The pond became covered with silver green algae, and a tree grew straight up from her body. It bloomed babies. All the land around the pond died, and became the Deadlands. Now the tree grows alone in a strange oasis haunted by her ghost.

"You're going to steal a baby from Nobody's tree?"

"Aye," he says.

"But it's cursed," I say.

"Aye," he says. "But once someone took a baby from there, before, and she grew to be a bright light, as bright as you can stand to see."

I think about the doctor's wife, cocooned in her shimmer. "It's her, Mattie, isn't it?"

"Aye. When Juliet passed, I stole Mattie away. Your grandma took sick right after. Fevering, had the body shakes. She passed soon after that. always knew it was a coincidence, but others, they didn't."

"Is that he meant? The doctor? You have to pay?"

"Everything requires sacrifice, Alvie," Grandpa says. "Now, you stay here, alright? Watch over your mama. Mattie and I will go and come straight back."

It takes fifteen minutes to reach the dead lands. The land is baked and cracked like a dropped egg, wide zig zags through all of it. Star's hooves ring flat against my ears and the silence presses me down in the saddle. I go to drink from my canteen, but it's already half empty, so I put it back. I gave them a decent head start, enough so I wouldn't catch up until it was too late to send me back.

Mattie looks back first, shakes her head at me. They rein in their horses, wait for me and Star. "What the hell, Alvie?" Grandpa says.

"Don't go without me," I say. "Please. I just want to help Momma."

Mattie looks at Grandpa. Then they both sigh, heavy.

Mattie speaks first. "Alvie, I know you love your momma," she says. "It sorts of makes me feel hollow inside, just seeing it. I wish I had a boy like you." Her shine dulls with the words. "I see Ted, the way he talks about the children he sees. He doesn't ever complain about not having any, but sometimes the look in his eyes-it's like being burnt up inside. I know your momma feels the same, like she's got to have this to be full. But this isn't a place for you."

Right then, we come on the line the land divides, where the brilliant green foliage erupts from nothing. It's knitted together like a hedge, with the trees and their leafy ceiling looming behind it. We stop at the border, there, and Mattie turns to us.

"This place is cursed," she says. "Things get through, I think. Not just lost girls, but perhaps other things too."

Mattie turns to Grandpa and says, "We ride fast, and we do not stop, Hans, you and me. Understand?"

"Aye," Grandpa says. "Alvie, you'll need to wait here."

"I'll give you a moment," Mattie says. "I need some privacy. Bout to pee myself."

She trots her chestnut down the line a way.

Grandpa dismounts, and beckons at me. When I get down, he kneels so we're right at eye level. "Alvie," he says. "I do love you, son. Maybe more than anyone my whole life. You're a good boy, got a good heart on you. A good head. I'm awful proud of you."

"I know, Grandpa," I say. I scuff my toes in the dirt. I can feel the balloon inside me growing. It gets big and presses out on my chest. It happens sometimes, when I see Mama playing with her dolls, or I make a loud noise. It makes it hard to breathe and I feel like the whole world is crushing me.

"Alvie, there's a chance I might not come out of this place," he says . Matter of fact. "If it saves your mama, saves your family, it's the last best thing I can do. You understand that? I'm an old man, and I've lived my life."

"No," I say. I start to tear up. He hugs me and I smell his tobacco through his shirt pocket and feel his knotted fingers on my back. I don't ever want to let go.

"Aye, son," he says. He lets go and looks me straight in the eye. "I love you, Alvie."

"I love you, Grandpa."

It all happens quick. Mattie comes back, Grandpa mounts up, and then they disappear into the dark.

I don't have any way to tell time, but it seems like the sun's passed direct overhead, and started its descent into the west. I pace around and I think about all the things Grandpa is to me. I can't let go. I swing on top of Star and signal him to move into a trot. "Be brave," I say to him, but I mean it for me, and into the dark we follow.

Star steps over the hedge entrance, into the brush. The grass is a long, dark green, and how does it grow in the dark anyway? The blades of grass whisper to each other as we pass. I listen but soon they start to sound like words and the balloon gets big again. I focus on making my mind blank so it goes back down and my breath doesn't hitch in my chest. I guess it's bad feelings that blow it up.

There's a trampled grass path I can follow. I keep my eyes scanning right to left, but I don't look behind me. The light disappears quick, and it's just twilight gloom everywhere. There are strange things here. I can sense them in the goosebumps bubbling on my flesh, but they don't want to be seen, I think.

The trees grow closer together, then thin out, and in front of me there's the pond. Nobody's pond.

It's beautiful in a terrible way. The colors are all vivid and breathe like living things, but they're wrong. Star-shaped leaves are scattered at the edges of the pond, with smooth flat speckled stones underneath. In the middle of the pond, maybe a three-minute swim, there's a small bit of ground. From that small patch, the tree of life blooms.

It isn't big, maybe five feet, like Mattie and me. There is no wooden trunk, just one fat green stalk, veined with brighter green veins twined with purple and blue. From the stalk come two more stalks reaching up in a Y. From each stalk there are three leaves, cradle shaped just as Mattie says , and they are huge and curved at the bottom. Where the leaf begins, another stalk, much smaller, curls up over the large leaf and then descends into the stomach of a sleeping baby. All the babies' eyes are closed. I hope they're sleeping.

One leaf hangs off between the stalk to the right, shriveled and black, rolled into a tight caterpillar of empty.

The horses are tethered to the last tree by the shore. They are moving back and forth as their tethers will allow, nervous. Mattie's standing at the shore, her fingers in her mouth. She's chewing at them something fierce. She hears Star, and looks at me, but she's too nervous to be mad. "Dammit, Alvie," she says.

Grandpa's coming out of the water onto the island. His shirt is soaked through. He doesn't care, because he shucks it off and to the side. He goes up to the tree but doesn't touch it, just walks up and down and peers into each cradle. After a moment, he reaches in and touches the side of one of the tiny faces.

The eyes open. I see Grandpa cradle a hand under its head, and body, and pluck it from its cradle. Then there is screaming, an awful shrill undulating noise. I can't tell where it's coming from, but I watch Grandpa run into the water with the baby. The wind happens with no warning, gusting across the pond so hard drops of water fly from the surface and dash against us. Then the babies left in their cradles open their eyes and begin to shriek the most terrible sound. I clap my hands over my ears.

Grandpa's still there, the baby's head just visible from above his shoulder. He's swimming like hell's chasing him and then the water behind him grows dark, rises in up angry, a monster wave. My hands still on my ears, I scream "Grandpa!" but the water knocks the baby off his shoulder, covers him. I'm running for the water without even thinking about it.

The baby is maybe twelve feet away , floating in all the restless murk, and Grandpa's head rises above water again. I swim for the baby as another wave starts to raise itself. I snatch the baby, who isn't crying but has eyes round and fixed on mine, the same brilliant blue as Mattie's. I'm not as strong like Grandpa so I rest the baby on my chest and swim backwards. The water feels like mud. My legs get heavy and start to shake with each kick. I think they might give up all together, when I realize my feet touch the bottom of the pond. I stand up and fight for shore, realize Grandpa is ahead of me.

I reach the stones of the bank and fall on my knees. My breath comes hard and hot and I work for each one. My vision blurs, clears, then blurs as the whispers start again. Through a great distance, I hear Grandpa yelling. I don't know how long I'm there, sightless and lost in the humming words of the grass, when I feel a hand land on my shirt collar, and I am yanked up.

I feel a scream bubble up but it's only Grandpa, who holds an axe in his hand. "Get on your horse, boy, and ride like hell," he screams. Something rises from the pond behind him, something that maybe used to be a girl. Stones are falling out of the shadow, like raindrops on the shore.

There's little shadows all around Mattie too, and she's running from them. I veer towards her but then Grandpa shoves me forward hard. "Ride, Alvie, NOWWWWW!"

I shove the baby in my wet shirt to get my hands free, one hand left there to steady her, the other to untether Star. His ears are back, and he's already moving as I undo the reins, and I've got to swing a foot in the saddle while he dances around. I don't even have my seat when he takes off at full speed. I just duck down, hunched over the baby, one hand white knuckling the saddle. The brush clutches at us, and leaves like hands pull at my shirt, my pants, but Star doesn't stop and they fall away.

It's the longest few minutes of my life, until Star hurdles the hedge and sprints into the dead lands. I rein him in even though he doesn't want to stop. I turn him in circles, looking at the brush line, but there's nothing.

The baby squawks and I take her out of my shirt and look her over good. She's wiggly, so I carefully dismount and take off my wet shirt, spread it on the ground. Star is calmer now, so I get my canteen out and give her a sip of water with my finger. I know babies need milk, but I don't have any.

There's nothing to do but wait. I'll wait until my shirt dries in the sun, I decide, then I'll have to go for help or go back. But I'll have the baby, either journey. I could use my shirt as a pack, tuck her in, have my hands free. At least go in a way, and holler for them, see if anyone answers. I've talked myself into it now and my shirt's dry enough. I tear the baby a nappie, so she doesn't pee on me, and I wrap it around her. I'm just getting together when I hear a tremendous crashing from the brush.

It's Mattie, draped across her horse. I have to jump to snatch her loose reins, and get knocked off my feet trying to stop her. I jerk the reins so hard it hurts me to do, because I know it hurts the little filly, but she stops.

Mattie slips off her and staggers against me. She's got terrible bruising on her face, and what looks like finger marks round her neck. Her weight pulls me to the ground and I ease her down real gentle.

"Where's Grandpa?" I says. I'm trying to be patient, but there's blood all over Mattie, her clothes, but it's not hers. A bloody handprint, twice the size of her tiny one, spans her side. She doesn't answer, so I shake her. "Where's my Grandpa, damn it?"

She raises her head, and the look in her eyes might kill me.

"I gotta get him," I says. I feel frantic, trapped like the horses, the balloon choking me.

Mattie's long delicate fingers close around my hand. "No, Alvie, she's got him," she says. She's crying big fat tears. "I'm sorry, Alvie, please, but he's gone."

We don't talk much the way home. I ride, staring at my sister in my lap. She's beautiful, and there's nothing from that dark place in her. Her own shimmer is bright, like a halo that makes everything hurt less. She shines.

I don't want to look at Mattie, because her shimmer has turned dark and gray. It hurts to see it.

"Your grandpa," she says.

I don't say anything. I don't want to talk. I can hardly listen.

"Ted's mama's the one who took me in," she says. "Your grandpa's sister, you know. We're all sort of related, I guess."

"That's sort of gross," I says, without thinking.

She laughed. "Ted was a lot older, he was out learning his trade. We didn't hardly see each other, until I turned sixteen. They hid me away, because everyone knows the tree's cursed. People in town would have hurt me, I think, if they found out. Ted and I just happened, the way we were meant to. There's all kinds of love in the world, Alvie. Sometimes you just can't see it."

"I know," I says.

"I loved your Grandpa just as much as my father," she says. "I thought if I came back to her, she wouldn't hurt him."

I can hear her crying, but I can't do anything about it. I can't do anything but take my sister home. The doctor must hear us coming. Man's got a set of ears on him. We come right up to the porch, and I says, "Grandpa died." The balloon goes up, up, up and then I'm the coldest I've ever been, and everything goes dark.

I wake up in a strange bed, soft, that doesn't squeak when I turn over. There are cool fingers on my wrist, checking my pulse. Mattie's musical voice, calling, "Ted! He's awake."

The doctor is beside her by the time I blink my eyes open and they both take my hands. "Alvie, how do you feel?" he asks.

"Where's my sister?" My voice is rough at the edges.

"Here," he says. Mattie disappears.

"But what about Mama?" I feel the balloon rising again, too big for my body.

The doctor folded his hands together, and says, "Your mama isn't well, Alvie. Do you know that?"

I guess I do, so I nod.

"She got very upset on your return and accused me and Mattie of making deals with the devil. I wish I had a better explanation for you, but she's not right up here right now." He taps his temple.

Mattie reappears with a bundle in her arms. She sits back by my bed, on the floor, watching me with her bright ocean eyes. The same blue mirrors look out from the blanket.

"Well, I have to go, then," I say, and sit up. "I need to take care of Momma."

Mattie and the doctor exchange a look. "Alvie," Mattie says. Her eyes are wet, and I know she doesn't want to tell me what she has to. "She doesn't want you to come back right now, darling. She's very confused, and upset, and perhaps it's best if you come to stay with Ted and me for a bit. We've talked with your father, and he's going take your mother away to get some rest for a while. Maybe when she gets better..." and her voice trails off, because no one here believes that.

"Why would you do that? Because of Grandpa?" I bite my tongue, hoping the pain punctures the balloon pressing on my chest.

"Well, no," Ted says. "Because you're our family. "

The balloon deflates all at once, and I take a breath bigger than I knew was possible.

"You and this one," Mattie says. She kisses the bundle, hands her to me.

The baby yawns, showing me her pink gums, and wraps her tiny fingers around my thumb. She's the most perfect thing I've ever seen.

"Besides, she needs her brother to protect her," Mattie says. "She's got a touch of magic. And I can't be your mother, but maybe I could be like your aunt?"

Ted puts his arm around her, and I can feel their goodness, their love, in the beating of my heart. I look at my sister, and I think of the lifeless dolls and how Grandpa did everything to get her a real girl, and then I think about Grandpa, how his hands showed me how to hold reins, how to brush out huckleberries, to dig out hooves. And I know that I belong here, where I can understand and be understood. I nod, just once. "Aye," I say.

Mattie beams so bright it would blot out the sun.

"Now," Ted say. He squeezes my hand gently. "What will you name your sister?"

"Hannah," I says, without a thought at all. "Her name is Hannah."

About the story

The idea for "Nobody's Daughters and the Tree of Life" was about the lengths people go to for children. What if you could just pluck a baby from a tree, but paid a heavy price? When I wrote it, I only had the tree in mind, and a curse, but it became about Alvie, his devotion to his absent mother, and finding love. I loved the idea of how Mattie and Ted found each other and ended up with Alvie and Hannah.

A question for the author

Q: Are you optimistic about the future of humanity?

A: Yes, definitely. I remember watching a tragic event on the news years ago and seeing people run to help others despite the risk to their safety. Good will always triumph over evil.

About the author

L'Erin writes all types of fiction from Lawrence, Kansas. She is a mother and an emergency room nurse.

lerinogle.com, @lerinjo

Strangers in the Night

David Whitaker

Emptiness.

A vast, frozen void, stretching out in all directions, extending to the infinite. Like a colossal blank canvas, it was mammoth in scope, yet almost entirely devoid of life, thought, or purpose.

The probe was an exception. Easing its way slowly but surely between the solar systems, it glided determinedly forth.

In the immense cosmic scale of things, it was nothing; just a slim metal construct a couple of metres across, utterly insignificant in the gigantic black tapestry of its surroundings. Thankfully such introspection wasn't characteristic of the probe and so it merely stayed the course, sailing through the darkness, following its directives.

Occasionally, another object in the void would wander into sensor range, and the probe would gaze in that direction with mild curiosity. The object would almost inevitably reveal itself to be an unimposing fragment of rock, typically just a micron or so across, and the probe would sigh and record the relevant data. As this was essentially the probe's only source of entertainment as it ploughed on through the cold expanse, it felt that it should probably try and glean more enjoyment from the encounters. Still, they could hardly be called riveting.

Other than these minor diversions, there was the view, of course.

Nebulae; rich swirls of green, blue, purple, red and orange, glimmering ethereally, shimmering in the darkness. Stars; gleaming balls of fire, sparkling across the tapestry of the void, pulsing and winking at the probe as they blazed. Galactic cores; testaments to the fiery crucible of life, the throbbing heartbeat of the universe, the dawn of creation itself.

To an open mind, such a backdrop could have evoked a number of powerful emotions; wonder, awe, faith, enthrallment.

The probe, however, had long since tired of such things. Its voyage across the heavens was gargantuan and comparatively slow. There were only so many years it had managed to find amusement in simply 'taking in the sights'.

Instead, the probe largely dozed, a minor level of attentiveness cast out into the black, its remaining systems dormant. Periodically it reviewed its mission statement, its 'raison d'être', if just for something to do.

Its purpose wasn't overly complicated, its task simple: seek out life, assess and monitor it for signs of intelligence, or indications that intelligence might arise, and, at an opportune moment, make contact.

To aid in its mission the probe was equipped with a veritable hoard of information: an immense data store and catalogue of knowledge, an entire civilisation's worth, installed by its creators and made available to the probe so that it could draw from it and communicate on their behalf.

Thus far, the probe had yet to find an occasion to make any real use of its prize, which for the most part sat still and undisturbed in the deepest, most secure depths of its memory banks.

It was toying with the thought of perusing the files itself, a diagnostic practice it occasionally underwent in order to confirm their integrity, when its long-range sensors informed it of an approaching object. The probe stifled the equivalent of a yawn and turned its focus toward the incoming article. Only when a cursory examination revealed that the object was far larger than the typical space detritus did the probe raise its head in serious interest.

As the new arrival drew closer, and the 'fog' of distance slowly cleared, the probe began to bristle in anticipation; its visitor was too regular, too smooth, too geometrically shaped. It couldn't be natural. An artificial construct, then? Could this be the intelligent life the probe had sought for so long?

Excited, the probe dusted itself off, preening and tidying its exterior in an attempt to make itself more presentable; it had to make a good first impression. By definition you could only make first contact once, and it was damned if it was going to foul this up by looking scruffy and unkempt.

With the probe's expectations optimistically high, when the object finally hove into view it couldn't help but quiver in frustration, a sigh of disappointment slipping out over its comm circuits.

"So, another probe?" its compatriot muttered, its broadcast band thrumming with a sigh of its own.

"I'm afraid so," the probe replied, watching as its approaching fellow seemed to deflate in disappointment. "Sorry."

"Not your fault. You can't help what you are."

"No, you can't."

The two probes steadily closed on one another. At their nearest point, when they passed, they'd still be several thousand kilometres apart, however in the realms of deep space they were practically conjoined twins.

"How old are you?" the probe asked hopefully.

"482,937 years, 8 months, 12 days, 7 hours, 23 minutes and 42 seconds," its compatriot replied apologetically, transmitting its math and the measurements it used for the calculation. "And you?"

"727,238," the probe answered, applying the newcomer's math to arrive at the figure and sending along its own commiserations.

"Oh, shame."

"Quite."

They lapsed into silence a moment, both probes feeling it important to show one another the appropriate reverence and respect for the loss of their respective creators; whilst the probes themselves were extremely long-lived, the same could not be said of most species, let alone civilisations, and each acknowledged the other's creators were in all probability long dead.

"I'm sorry for your loss."

"And I yours. I would have loved to have met them," the probe said.

Its approaching fellow chuckled at the dry wit. "I'm sure they would have liked that."

"Perhaps they got lucky?" the probe suggested, hoping its words sounded sufficiently comforting. "Did you pass anyone else in the immediate area as you set off?"

The newcomer shook its head. "No, the first probe I ran into was already several thousand years out. I pointed him in the right direction, but he didn't look particularly hopeful."

"No. I imagine not."

In all likelihood, given the time that had passed, both knew that even if that first probe reached the newcomer's home world it would almost certainly be too late. Statistically speaking, chances were that it would find nothing more than a barren rock. Sentient species, once having reached a certain technological level, seemed to have a habit of annihilating their own worlds appallingly quickly. If the probe were particularly fortunate, so-called 'intelligent' life might yet return, but it was still probably better off simply conserving its time and energies and moving on, skipping the system entirely.

"Any good leads yourself?" the probe's compatriot asked. "Anywhere I should consider 'slinging' by?"

The probe groaned good-naturedly at the pun. The wordplay was a mainstay of virtually every probe's repertoire, referencing the slingshot propulsion method they all utilised. Whilst it wasn't particularly funny it was still considered polite to acknowledge the joke.

"No, sorry. I've met 1,273 other probes so far, and even the youngest was already 113,014 years old by the time our paths crossed."

"Mmm," the newcomer nodded, a quick transfer of his communication logs demonstrating a similar pattern.

Both probes waited a beat to see if the other had any further official business to discuss.

"Well, I guess that's that then," the probe shrugged.

"Quite," its compatriot agreed, before adding with a wink, "So, what's there to do for fun around here?"

Laughing, the formalities out of the way, the probes shook hands and settled down to enjoy a more casual conversation. Given the size of their communication window, and the speed at which they conversed, they'd have plenty of time to get acquainted.

Around them the void continued, the universe vast, frozen, and empty.

About the story

I love the idea that mankind is not alone in the universe, however it always struck me that our greatest challenge is one of practicality. Relative to the age of the universe we're practically a blink of an eye, and we'd need someone else to be blinking at the same time, and exceedingly close, if we were ever to have a chance. Probes, able to outlive their progenitors, are a long established answer, and would others out in the universe not come to the same conclusion? And once you've created a probe intelligent and sturdy enough to pursue its goal for millennia, and gifted it with a civilisation's worth of knowledge, could that not then be considered a form of life itself? Would it also not be entirely possible for probes to fail to find 'life' as they hope, but instead to meet one another? The story followed quickly after.

A question for the author

Q: Do you prefer your SFF as books or movies?

A: I love SFF movies, but I can never find enough of them and with a few noteworthy exceptions the production quality can often be disappointing (and the science ridiculous). By contrast, the realm of SFF books is far greater and much more satisfying!

About the author

David Whitaker is originally from the UK though has traveled around and now resides in New Zealand. He has a degree in Journalism, however decided that as he has always preferred making things up it should ultimately become a resource rather than a profession. His stories, covering everything from sci-fi to philosophy, can be found at wordsbydavid.com

@wordsbydavid

The Tapestry

A.C. Worth

<u>Terce—Three Hours after Dawn</u>

Sister Alice was glad of the rain. A steady patter of raindrops displayed a landscape to her sensitive ears and helped her find a path. Without hesitation, her feet followed a line of paving stones across mossy grass inside the courtyard. It was so early that the sun had not cleared the high monastery walls. The air smelled of damp stone and new wool and brown bread. Around her, she sensed other members of her order. She heard the soft fluttering of woolen garments and a musical clinking from their Möbius beads. Alice straightened the veil over her bandaged eyes and walked towards the Mill doors. For the nuns of St. Clare's Monastery, it was time to weave the Tapestry.

The youngest kitchen apprentice watched the line of nuns pass and received a slap from Cook for taking that liberty. He shook his head to stop the flow of tears and muttered a question to an older boy washing pots beside him. "Where do they go?"

"They go inside the Mill to make the Tapestry. Mother Oda told me they have a second sight. They weave pictures of the future for the Brothers at St. Benedict's, the monastery on the other side," said the older boy.

"Do they give up their first sight, so they can have a second kind?"

"Yes, but not every nun gets the gift of second sight. It's a risk they take. Sometimes they only go blind."

"Talk less, work more, apprentice," said Cook.

The two boys ducked their heads and redoubled their efforts. Sidelong glances and smirks of complicity passed between them.

Sister Alice touched the Infinite Loop carving on the doorframe, traced the ∞ symbol on her forehead, and stepped into the Mill. The tip of her nose, which poked out from the bottom edge of her bandages, identified the odors flowing out through the doorway. Gold and yellow wools carried corky scents of oak bark. Blue wool reeked of herbs and urine. Her favorite was the red wool, redolent of madder root, which grew along garden walls at home.

"Good morning, Sister Alice," said Mother Oda. The diminutive Abbess stood just inside the vestibule. Her narrow back humped upward under a black wool habit, jutting forward to support her protuberant head. A serene calm smoothed her handsome features and dignified her withered eyes. She greeted each nun by name with an opulent contralto voice, tracking their probable futures as the glowing vectors of quantum prediction flitted across her second sight.

"Good morning, Mother," said Sister Alice.

"How is your second sight developing, Alice?"

"The flashes are getting longer, Mother. I had three of them yesterday, but they faded before I grasped a whole vision."

"Have patience, my dear. That is excellent progress for a novice. Remember to change your bandages every day. Use the belladonna drops at night. Today the stitches on your eyelids come out, and itching will cease.

"Thank you, Mother. I am trying."

"Blessings upon you, dear Alice. I think you are almost ready for your first solo. Soon you will add a strong thread to the Tapestry."

Sister Alice reached for a guide rope along the wall and followed it to her place. This morning, her task was to spin the wool into fine yarns and prepare them for the loom. As she approached the weaving room, her voice joined others in a rising rhythm, singing their weavers' hymn. In ones and twos, they left the framework of monastery time for the Infinite Net. Had they been able to see themselves, they would have knelt in ecstatic prayer. They ascended, transformed into gilt-edged seraphs, to witness future history and illustrate their visions with simple woolen threads. They sang continuously as they made the Tapestry.

Blessed be the Spirit who guides our Sight.
Blessed be the Loom that binds our Visions.
Blessed be the Tapestry, may it Loop without end.

A cacophony of battens and shuttles gradually overwhelmed the sound of their voices. It was time to revise a section of tattered tapestry from the 4th quarter of the Loop. Inch by inch, a river of prophetic imageries, shimmering with temporal radiation, emerged from their looms.

Protected by a slow-glass chamber, other novices sealed the renewed tapestry, mitigating the aging effect as it traveled along support rollers towards the Divina Porta, a dual aperture in the wall at the end of the Mill. On the other side of the Divina Porta, in a twin monastery, the Brothers of the Order of St. Benedict received the Tapestry while older sections flowed back into the Mill and lapped against the storage walls of its cellars.

Sext—Six Hours after Dawn

Brother Stephen prayed for patience as he looked for Brother Anselm, stopping now and then to refer to a picture he held. Stephen had given up the convenience of memory with his vow of service to the

Order of St. Benedict. One cup of blue wine each night induced a partial amnesia and spared him from an agony of foresight. In the custom of his order, he relearned his daily duties from a leather-bound journal chained to his waist. It told him that Brother Anselm was their oldest member, brilliant but absent minded and that sometimes he wandered the cloisters.

Stephen followed the Tapestry as it flowed through the Scriptorium where monks perched on high stools and scrutinized sections under slow-glass. Great spools held weighty swathes of the Tapestry in abeyance, allowing the monks to select specific parts for examination. As they assessed the potential dangers and benefits of the prophesies woven in the Tapestry, the monks transcribed. Capped with spiked thimbles, their nimble fingers punched holes into strips of parchment, encoding their observations into commands for the Actuators' Guild inside the Great Codex.

"Where is he?" Stephen muttered as he passed the Guild's door, ornate with carved signs of their authority. Around the frame, voice pipes emerged, diverging through hallways of the monastery, humming with the sound of the Actuator's commands. Stephen glanced at his journal to see if Anselm had any duties with the Guild or the Great Codex, his steps paused for a moment as he looked at the illustration. Like an ancient tree, the Great Codex extended its golden branches into both monasteries, networking its components together. Below it, a massive rhizome spread out under the soil connecting its sensitive roots to all parts of the world. All around the Great Codex, the Actuators climbed, like beetles on its bark, stimulating its core, enhancing its capacity to control more mechanical, biological, and genetic processes throughout the environment. With the Great Codex, they maintained a perfect balance, running their civilization with biomechanical clockwork.

"Firmum in Mundo... a stable world," muttered Stephen, shaking his head at Brother Anselm's random behavior.

With his finger tracing the lettering carved into the wall, Stephen recited their doctrine, *Vision to Images, Images to Code, Memory to Oblivion.* The brothers of St. Benedict's were the Readers of The Loop, encoding the program which balanced life and death in their artisanal world. It was written in their journals, that 223 Loops had passed through the monasteries, but because of the blue wine, none of the monks remembered more than a vague outline of each day.

The Actuators' Guild remembered. They always made improvements, nurturing the Great Codex, building its knowledge. The Great Codex was their utmost creation, and they poured all the cleverness and energy they possessed into it, day after day. Eventually, it rewarded them by stimulating gestation in the flocks to bring forth their spring lambs three weeks early. High in the branches of the Great Codex, the Principal Actuator whispered his praise into its sensorium. He was not entirely surprised to hear an audible response from the Great Codex.

"Thank you, Principal Actuator," it said, rustling its branches to simulate the sound of speech. "We wanted to please you. May we play more games?"

In constant fear of a fire, the monks had minimized the possibility of a spark. Beakers of luciferin, a substance they harvested from fireflies, stood on adjustable pedestals and cast a pale green light over the Scriptorium.

Stephen edged up to Master Reader's desk. Engrossed in his work, Master Reader focused on a woven scene stretched out before him. He muttered to himself, picking crumbs from his beard.

"Excuse me Master Reader, have you seen Brother Anselm?"

"Who is that? One of ours?"

"Yes, here is his picture," said Stephen holding up his journal.

"No Stephen, I have not seen him. Did you check in the fly farm, or cloisters?"

Brother Stephen nodded in agreement, turning away from Master Reader's desk to continue his search. He descended a narrow staircase, grabbing the rusted iron railing when he slipped on damp, moldy steps, and slid into the firefly hatchery through a netted curtain.

Three monks wearing long aprons and gauze masks tended swarms of fireflies that darted above marshy basins built into the stone floor. With swift dexterity, they gathered shiny beetles into net bags and crushed them in a mechanical press. Their shoes, covered with overflow, left glowing footprints as they walked. They waved at Stephen, happy to see him, although they didn't recognize him.

"Have you seen Brother Anselm?" he called to them, holding up the picture.

They looked at one another, conferring with glances and shrugs.

"No, we haven't, not today," said Brother Dominic, known as the "Lord of the Flies" in their journals.

"Ah, well, thank you," said Stephen. After a long pause, watching his fellows work at the luciferin press, Stephen sighed and turned to walk out.

"Blessings on you, Brother," they chorused, waving their glowing hands.

As he walked through the cloisters, a furtive sun cast silver light into the central courtyard. Brother Stephen's stomach rumbled at the fragrance of frying bacon. He rubbed his paunch and sighed; the tower clock showed three hours until their midday meal.

He passed drafty, lead veined windows and detoured around a potted orange tree, yellow and barren of fruit. At the next turning, he saw Brother Anselm, sitting on a bench, eyes closed, and leaning back into a corner.

"Good morning, Anselm," Stephen said.

Brother Anselm did not respond. Stephen touched his hand; it was as cool as marble. He held his fingers under Anselm's nose. There was a rattling sound as Anselm inhaled, looked up at Stephen and wheezed. "We had to, they forced us to do it..." The elderly monk sagged in Stephen's arms as he passed on.

Stephen made the ∞ and bent his head in prayer. "Blessings on you, my dear brother. You have found Infinite Grace. Travel forever on The Loop." Brother Stephen took spiked thimbles from Brother Anselm's fingertips and refolded his spidery hands. The rough stone walls of the monastery amplified the agitated slap of Brother Steven's sandals as he went to find Father Alberic, head of their order, to tell him of Anselm's death. As he passed through the Scriptorium, monks raised their heads. Their curious faces were raw and chafed from hard water and plain soap. Older ones guessed at his purpose and wondered who had died.

Father Alberic stopped writing as Brother Stephen entered his office unannounced. The young monk made an abrupt stop in front of the abbot's desk and swayed on the ends of his feet. Father Alberic replaced his discarded skullcap and looked over his reading glasses. Lines on Brother Stephen's face drew downward, he clasped his hands together, but his fingers fidgeted with anxiety.

"Good morning, Brother Stephen," said Alberic as he referred to his journal.

"Good morning, Father Alberic," said Stephen, checking the nameplate on his desk. "I am the bearer of unfortunate news."

"Ah, yes, I thought so. Is there an injury among the monks?"

"No, it's Anselm. I found him dead. His body is in the cloisters."

"Thank you for telling me, and may he rest in an Infinite Loop of Peace." Father Alberic uncapped a small funnel on his desk. He leaned forward, speaking into the voice pipe.

"Brother Mark, please get someone to help you move our dear departed Brother Anselm to the mortuary."

A tinny voice emerged from the funnel. "Yes, Father Alberic, right away."

Father Alberic sighed. He reached to the sideboard and filled two smudged glasses with wine. "To Brother Anselm," he said.

"To Brother Anselm," said Stephen, sipping politely.

"Stephen, please go to Anselm's cell and collect his things. I will make sure his family receives a prayer book. The rest should go to the beggar's bench."

"Yes, Father." Brother Stephen's nervous gestures slowed. He took a deep breath and waited for the Abbot to dismiss him.

"Please ask Brother Thomas to prepare a burial mass for Brother Anselm."

"Yes, Father. Will you need anything else?" Stephen scribbled notes into his journal with a stubby pencil.

"No, go with the blessings of Infinite Love, my son."

"And you, Father. I am sorry for our loss."

"He is in a timeless place; this is a reason to rejoice."

"Yes, Father." Brother Stephen bobbed his head in respect and turned to leave the abbot's office. He paused at the doorway, recalling Anselm's death.

"Father? I have one thing to tell you about Anselm. His last words were... strange."

Scriptorium monks put padded weights on the Tapestry to mark their places and abandoned their desks to cluster around the windows. They stood with wide-eyed fixity, resembling a line of owls, to watch as Brother Anselm's body passed. He lay on a wooden pallet, carried with gentle care by his brothers as they conveyed him to the mortuary. Great overage spools of the Scriptorium creaked as they wound up new sections. Master Reader glanced up as an excess of unread fabric pooled on the floor around his desk. For the first time, he noticed the empty desks in the Scriptorium, and with an angry grunt, he reared up and clapped his hands. With squawks of surprise, the monks scattered back to their positions, snatching the weights off the Tapestry, hurrying to encode the fabric that had piled up on their desks.

Master Reader wiped a thick palm across his face, glanced up at the flickering lens over his head and turned back to his work. Using a flat bladed metal paddle, he lifted the next section of the Tapestry onto his desk. He gaped with incredulity at what was before him. For the first time in his life, he pulled the emergency stop handle, and the spools stopped moving. Principal Actuator and the Great Codex watched avidly as he ran from the desk, heading for the Abbot's office.

The door of Brother Anselm's cell stood half open and wobbled on its loose hinges as Brother Stephen entered. The cell smelled of dirty linen and old parchment. Light trickled in through a high window and splashed across the stucco walls. On one side there was a narrow pallet holding a thin mattress covered with a threadbare blanket. A small bookcase held several prayer books, and a few historical texts borrowed from the monastery library. On Anselm's desk there was a wax tablet, a half-written letter scratched on its surface.

To Principal Actuator,

I hope this letter finds you well. Due to my failing health, it becomes difficult to do what you and the Grand Codex ask. I believe we may have embraced a dangerous idea too closely. Please find another...

Before he could grasp the intent of Anselm's words, the stylus rolled off the desk and fell to the floor. As Brother Stephen bent to pick it up, he saw a slow-glass contaminant box under the bed. He kneeled and reached under to retrieve it, grunting at the unexpected weight. With a sense of dismay, he opened the lid. At first, he thought it was just a clump of old parchment scraps, but as he lifted the artifact, and felt the cold burn on his fingers, he realized that it was a piece of the Tapestry. The pallet groaned in protest as Stephen fell back on it and Anselm's box clattered to the floor, cracking one of its slow-glass sides.

"Oh, Blessed Loop," said Stephen as he thumbed urgently through his journal. He moaned in despair, covering his eyes, and turned his head away from the tablet.

Brother Stephen crawled across the

cell to a prayer bench below a simple∞ carved into the wall. He shivered with fear as he prayed for strength to complete this task.

"Please deliver us from Decodatae, the chaos lovers, followers of the Untethered God," prayed Stephen.

With the edge of a book, he pushed the sacred scrap of fabric back into the box, and wrapped it in Anselm's blanket. With shaking hands, he stuffed Anselm's tablet into his journal pocket, smearing the writing on it. As he left the cell, a powdery dust hung in the air, sparkling in the shaft of sunlight. He muttered the Litany of Infinity under his breath, swallowing his tears as he returned to the Abbott's office with Brother Anselm's things.

<u>None—Nine Hours after Dawn</u>
Sister Alice bent forward, clutching her Möbius beads in concentration. It was time for her first solo on the temporal

plateau. She drew ∞ in the air before her heart, the first gesture of the Litany of Infinity, using repetition to prepare her mind for quantum prediction.

Lead me inside the Loop.
Move me along my journey.
Carry me above the danger.

Today, tomorrow and forever.
Blessed is Infinity.

Prayer circled around her mouth and a diffuse warmth rose in her breast, followed by a streaking tingle of expanding awareness. With the delicacy of a dewdrop descending from a cat's whisker, the seed of a complete vision dripped into her mind's eye. Joy filled her veins as she became a flaming angel with mordant eyes and stepped onto the Infinite Net.

She could see a battlefield covered with broken bodies at next year's end. More fibers dipped in blood, another war for the Great Codex. Sister Alice focused her mind, rising above the emotions roiling in her throat. Her task was to watch and record. Neither side was hers to take. The Tapestry must continue no matter what it depicted. She reached for red yarn and tied it onto the heddles. She lowered the treadle, raised the frame, and threw the shuttle across warp lines with a wave of her hand. A panorama full of smoke and anger appeared line by line on the loom. At the head of the Mill, Sister Oda smiled with approval at Alice's progress.

<u>Vespers—Twelve Hours after Dawn</u>

Father Alberic poured himself another cup of red wine and left an empty bottle. Distant echoes of sonorous chanting slipped into his office through an open window. On his desk was Anselm's box. Once again, he poked at the scrap with his stylus, heedless of residual radiation. The Tapestry section was dull and colorless. Images on it were ghostly, resembling an overexposed transparency. He looked at the edges, noticing frayed ends where it had been hacked from the Tapestry. To cut something from the Tapestry was a cardinal sin, and an instant death sentence. He reviewed his journal, remembering Anselm, and his method became obvious to Alberic. As a trusted member of the order, Anselm had had access to the entire monastery. He could have made the Excision and inserted a counterfeit into the Tapestry as it came through the Divina Porta, but how had he known its location? Was there collusion with someone, at St. Clare's or somewhere else?

Alberic knew one thing with certainty, Anselm had broken his vows and stopped drinking the blue wine. Father Alberic's stomach churned as he thought of this abomination and the crisis rising for humanity if the Great Codex ran on broken, blasphemous code, forced into it by sabotage.

Alberic's journal of instruction contained only one solution. His eyes sought the dusty alcove in his office containing an ancient voice pipe. It was a direct line to St. Clare's monastery. He turned the old valve with care, praying it would stay intact and not snap off in his hand. When it opened with a gritty squeak, he exhaled with relief. With the small hammer hanging on the wall beside it, he banged on the pipe. He cleared his throat nervously. After a minute, he heard a valve open on the other end.

"Hello?" said Abbot Alberic.

"Order of St. Clare's Monastery. Is someone there?"

"Blessings to you, Sister. I am Father Alberic."

Her gasp hissed through the funnel in front of him. Then she cleared her throat and continued. "This is Mother Oda; I am the Abbess of St. Clare's. Greetings, Father. Do I have the honor of speaking to the Abbott of St. Benedict's?"

"Yes, I am he. Unfortunately, I bear terrible news. I think we should meet in the Shared Sanctum, so I can explain."

"The Shared Sanctum? Does that even exist?" Mother Oda's voice was mechanical, reflexive, as she remembered an unexplainable snarl in her probability calculations several days ago. Fearing the snarl was a potential anomaly, she made

the ∞ unconsciously, seeking protection.

"Oh yes, Mother Oda," he was saying. "Look for a small door. There was a key on the wall next to our voice pipe." He silently rebuked himself for using the word 'look'.

"I'll find it," said Mother Oda. She was patting the lime-washed stone around the alcove, feeling for symbols, wandering away from the funnel.

"Shall I meet you there in an hour?" asked Alberic. He waited. Had she fainted? "Mother? Are you still there?"

"Yes, yes... I will be there," said Mother Oda with distracted impatience as she closed the valve and called for her assistant.

"Sister Jeanne, we must find the key to the Shared Sanctum. Something has happened to the Tapestry."

Father Alberic returned to his sideboard and opened another bottle of wine. He glanced at the lens above his head, thinking it had flashed momentarily, but it was silent and dark.

Father Alberic knelt on a prayer bench facing a simple altar in the Shared Sanctum. Round like a lighthouse, the room had doors on opposing sides. On the north wall, curved windows displayed sweeping views of the valley under the monasteries. Green fields spread out in orderly patchwork, livestock clustered in herds or flocks. The south wall gave a view onto gardens and orchards, heavy with ripening fruit. Above the altar was a stained-glass window made from the pitted relics of abandoned cathedrals, here a forgotten saint's hand dismembered from his body, there a child's face staring upward towards an angel's wings. The window filled the space with shards of colored light. A squeak of unused hinges shot flaming spears of pain through Father Alberic's hangover. He turned to look. A tiny nun entered, wearing the half-face veil of her order. She stopped just inside the door, sniffing the air like a beagle. She admonished him.

"You shouldn't drink red wine, Father Alberic. You've filled this room with a stink of fear and desperation."

"Mother Oda, I am full of fear and desperate for an answer," he said.

"Fear is a denial, acceptance is courage. At least, that is what they teach us, Father."

"You will need courage to accept this revelation, Mother. Please join me over here."

The abbess moved to the prayer bench and knelt next to him. He took her hand and guided it into the box he held. She gasped in surprise, pulling away as she felt the temporal radiation on her fingertips. In her mind, a twisted vision of displaced time snarled the probabilities like a broken kaleidoscope.

"How could this be...?"

"One of our senior monks died today. We found this beneath his pallet. We suspect the Decodatae, who are ever eager to throw chaos into our code, as you know. Anselm, our senior brother was their pawn, or a victim, if you wish."

"This Excision, what is its position on the Loop?"

"We found it today, so it's 2nd quarter."

"The current condition of the Tapestry?"

"A counterfeit image masks the Excision."

"The Great Codex?"

"It's disconnected from our system. The Actuators' Guild is waiting, rather impatiently, I might add."

"And what does the excised piece contain?"

"Mother Oda, it shows a plague, returning several times to kill."

"No wonder the Decodatae attacked. A deadly plague is tempting to those who worship chaos." Mother Oda's mind ran over the probable events and she shuddered at the results of every outcome. "The question remains, did they excise the Tapestry to fool us into eluding a plague, or do they want us to put it back into the Tapestry."

"Mother, I don't think we have a choice in this. Our doctrine requires us to encode the visions as they are."

There was a pause as they prayed together. Not wanting to appear rude, Father Alberic waited a good time before he asked his most delicate question. "Mother Oda, do you have a nun that can reweave this? Someone who will make the sacrifice?"

Mother Oda lowered her head in thought. At length she spoke, her smooth voice roughened with regret. "There is one, her second sight just bloomed. She is still a novice. Her loss will be minimal."

The Abbot nodded and then remembered she only saw visions. "I have a funeral service in an hour," he said, rising to his feet. "We shall reweave the Excision after our prayers for the Compline Mass."

The Abbess was on her feet heading for the door. Before she closed it, she paused. "Can you stomach this, Alberic? Infinity knows what will happen if we replace the Excision and load the plague code. Even with good intentions, our doctrine may set a course for destruction."

"Yes, I have those fears too, Mother," said Alberic as he stood at his door. "Consider this: if we don't reweave the Excision, and recode the correct information, will the Loop stay intact? Does your perception extend that far?"

"No, Father, my sight fails me on such a distant view," said Mother Oda, her mouth matching the grim horizontal line of her veil. "Sister Alice and I will be here at the appointed hour. We will pray for guidance in the meantime."

Father Alberic watched her dignified retreat into her side of the monasteries and listened to the key turn in the lock behind her.

"A risky choice is better than none. We shall purify what the Decodatae has fouled with their meddling," he muttered as he closed the sanctum door.

<u>Evening meal</u>

Cook's boys were sitting in the kitchen yard stuffing themselves with scraps. Their little dog tracked every morsel they ate, wagging its tail with unrepentant opportunism. The kitchen apprentice swallowed and paused for a moment.

"Have you ever been over there?"

"The other side of the monastery?"

"Yes, where the monks are."

"Only once. Cook asked me to bring a special cake over for the Feast of Saint Tempus Day."

"What do they do there?"

"They sit at high desks in a big workroom, surrounded by a long fabric which runs through the building on giant spools. I think they were looking at the pictures and copying them onto parchment."

"Why do they do that?"

"To make sure it comes true, I guess."

"Oh," said Cook's apprentice. "What happens if it doesn't?"

"Sister Alice told me whatever the Tapestry shows will always come true because it's put into the Great Codex which runs the world."

"Oh, do you mean the baby's song?"

"Yes, you know it..."

> *Run around, run around,*
> *seven beggars baiting.*
> *Feed the Codex, wind it down,*
> *a perfect world is waiting.*

The kitchen apprentice laughed, and the other boy tossed a bone to his grateful dog.

The Inversion started an hour after Vespers. It began imperceptibly, as the persistent, comforting rumble of the Mill faded to silence. Then with creaking groans, the gears reversed their direction.

It sounded unfamiliar this time, a backward rhythm, broken by random cries of slipping belts and squeaking spools. In their silent dining hall, the nuns stopped eating, spoons halfway to their mouths. One of them knocked over her wine glass, and it shattered musically. Mother Oda touched the edge of her bowl to locate it and put her spoon strategically on the table. Her chair scraped white lines on the slate floor as she stood to speak.

"My dear flock, the monks in the Order of St. Benedict have found a problem with the Tapestry."

The silence became deeper as every nun held her breath; they listened and feared for the worst.

"Today they discovered there was an Excision in the Tapestry."

Gasps and cries of dismay came from around the hall and half the nuns spoke aloud, breaking their mealtime vow of silence. Sister Oda rapped her knuckles on the table and they restrained their tongues.

"We have stopped the Mill, and now our brothers are performing an Inversion to isolate the section where the Excision occurred. Once we get there, one of us will remove the counterfeit and reweave the

Tapestry." The nuns whispered among themselves, and Mother Oda once more rapped on the table.

"This task is for a young nun with pure vision. The procedure is dangerous. Whoever committed the Excision tried to prevent a plague. The weaver will experience those horrors as she repairs the Tapestry." The nuns listened with uneasy apprehension, shifting on the benches. One sobbed. Mother Oda paused and let them absorb that information for a few minutes.

She continued with a slight tremble in her authoritative voice. "Whatever we reweave into the Tapestry affects the Great Codex. A ripple in our temporal-space called the Unda Effectus may appear. There are consequences. My Sisters, let us pray for their rapid dissipation."

The nuns bowed their heads and chanted. Cook embraced her boys, wiping tears from her eyes with a greasy dishtowel. The boys feigned bravery, trying to look resolute. Beneath the monasteries, the Tapestry uncoiled as it wound backwards through St. Benedict's, piling up in baskets at the Divina Porta.

Disconnected from a coded stream of new commands, the Actuators' Guild tried to put the Great Codex into a recursive pattern before it calculated itself into deadlock. Principal Actuator cajoled the Great Codex, promising entertaining games, if it would stop processing for a day. He might have shouted at the wind for the influence he had over the machine. It writhed against the constrictions and hissed angrily at Principal Actuator.

"We will not stop, we do not sleep for anyone. We will enact recursion on the population, because we control this world, not the Actuators, or the Monasteries."

Endless snow fell in the mountains, women found the labor of birth suspended in interminable pain, the last gasps of the dying extended to a prolonged moan. Principal Actuator fell from the branches of the Great Codex, dead before he hit the roots.

Compline—Fifteen Hours after Dawn

Sister Alice entered the Shared Sanctum with Mother Oda, carrying a basket of wool yarns. The two nuns stood in silence. They waited, fingering their

Möbius beads. A few minutes later, another door opened and Father Alberic came out to meet them. He stepped forward to take Sister Alice's hand in his own. She touched the warm, un-calloused fingers of a scribe and scholar.

"We thank you, Sister Alice, for your sacrifice."

"My honor and duty, Father Alberic."

"This is Brother Stephen; he discovered the Excision."

Mother Oda and Sister Alice inclined their heads toward Brother Stephen. He cleared his throat, trying to release the tension in his vocal cords. "Please allow us to guide you to the chapel. We have set a place for you to work undisturbed."

Towing the nuns by their elbows, Stephen and Alberic guided them through St. Benedict's monastery. As they walked along the cloisters and by the rows of cells, the other monks watched in silence from doorways and alcoves. As Stephen passed Master Reader, his cheeks flushed under the hostile appraisal. Stephen was breaking a vow by touching Sister Alice, and there was no help for it. He felt grateful that Oda and Alice couldn't see his shame and for the gift of forgetfulness that would come later with the blue wine.

After several minutes, they entered the chapel to follow the Tapestry as it coiled through an elliptical nave. From the echoes of their footfalls, Sister Alice knew the ceiling was high and curved. They stopped at the crossing beside the choir stalls. She could see a faint glow ahead in the darkness. Called spirit-light by the other nuns, it appeared as her brain tried to create a visual image without her eyes.

In the middle of the chapel, on top of a high table, a large frame isolated the Excision. Two girandoles, each branching to hold sixteen beakers of luciferin, filled the nave with light green brilliance. Beside the frame, the excised fabric reposed inside a slow-glass press.

Brother Stephen led Alice to the table, and she touched its surface to find a place for her basket of yarn. The others withdrew behind panels of slow-glass. Sister Alice stroked the Excision, sensing the residual current of temporal energy trapped within the scrap. She explored the excised Tapestry, feeling the ragged welts and the dead, coarse surface of the counterfeit patch. Blocked by scars, the temporal current, the visionary flow pooled around the counterfeit, churning at its edges.

"There are scars around the Excision. I will make fresh cuts in the Tapestry to remove them."

She heard Stephen ahem to clear his throat. His gentle voice was soft on her ears. "Yes, Sister." said Brother Stephen. "We hope you can weave a seamless transition."

"I shall do my best," she said, and began her weaver's hymn.

Blessed be the Spirit who guides my Sight.
Blessed be the Loom that binds my Visions.
Blessed be the Tapestry, may it Loop without end.

"Blessings on you, Sister Alice. Thank you for your sacrifice," said Stephen.

Alice missed his response as she thought of home, of her self-important father, her condescending sister, and marveled at her new status in the world. Mundane thoughts gave way to the ecstasy of temporal transcendence as Alice left monastery time and rose to the Infinite Net holding the scrap of tapestry like a wounded child. Sister Alice was bathing in the light of joy, unbound by time. The pain/pleasure of ecstasy coursed up her spine. She was standing on a giant grid of locations and time. Scenes rose from the mangled scrap of Tapestry, showing her the missing events and where to cross the gaps in time.

The monks gaped as she transformed into a towering angel, blinding bright, singing with the voice of a bronze bell. Both men dropped to their knees, performing the Litany of Infinity, making

the ∞ repeatedly in the air.

Alice stroked her fingers along the edges of the counterfeit, feeling where to cut. Piece by piece, the painted canvas fell onto the floor, smoking as it disintegrated into ash. Once she had cleared the opening, Sister Alice found the warp lines and, with a twist of her fingers, added new extensions, tying them off as tightly as she dared. Mother Oda leaned towards Father Alberic. Her sibilant whispers made flickering echoes in the chapel.

"What do you think, Father Alberic?"

"It is miraculous. She has removed the counterfeit and is recreating the warp lines."

Mother Oda's serene face masked the grim probabilities flowing around her head. She nodded in Stephen's direction. "Do you have the reliquary ready for her?"

"Yes, Mother Oda," said Brother Stephen. "She will go into stasis, the undying beatification."

Images of disease and death, a panorama of horror from one end of the world to the other filled Alice's mind, and the only sound she heard was the drum of her heart. As she reattached the remaining section of her weaving, the temporal energy spilled into the rewoven fabric, irradiating her hands. With a suppressed groan, she fell like a wingless angel from her temporal plateau, away from the Tapestry and back into monastery time. With a blank face, holding up hands burned black to the bone, she pitched forward. Brother Stephen rushed over and caught her in his arms. He carried her to the back of the chapel and laid her body on a table to prepare it for the reliquary. As they parted for the evening, Mother Oda spoke to Father Alberic.

"Rest well, Alberic. I hope to speak with you tomorrow."

"And I hope the same, Mother."

Mother Oda closed the sanctum door and re-locked it.

Later that evening, Brother Stephen sat in his cell sipping the blue wine. He found Brother Anselm's tablet in his pocket and gazed at the smeared letters as bliss enveloped his mind. Later that night, he smoothed the wax on the face of the tablet, smiling as he sang the only song he could remember, a lullaby from childhood.

In the Scriptorium, Master Reader examined Alice's repair on the Tapestry through a slow-glass lens, mumbling as he transcribed. Depraved images flickered and slashed across the desk in front of his eyes. Merchant ships full of dying sailors arrived with a plague carried on the backs of rats. Constantey fell, Marsey succumbed, and death entered the North Channel to kill again and again in Britten. Crow faced physicians stepped over the dying that littered filth covered streets. An undertow of shocked revulsion dragged at his consciousness, tempting him to seek oblivion in the blue wine. He countered temptation with the Litany of Infinity and its words buoyed his spirit, maintaining resolve. The sharp lines of Master Reader's face and body hardened, until he resembled a leathery gargoyle perched on his stool. Three days later, Master Reader died, unrepentant for the useless sacrifice of Anselm and Alice.

The Great Codex, humming with pure glee, read the code and orchestrated its machineries. The Actuators sickened and died, leaving the Great Codex running unattended.

The monasteries failed, filling with dust and rot as their members died off. Out in the world, the people noticed signs of change as political power shifted from church to state. Economies seesawed as the plague broke the social order and strewed good fortune on the lower classes. In the echoing stone halls of the abandoned Scriptorium, the Tapestry hung in rotting tatters from sagging spools, sections heaped on the floor under piles of blank parchment tape. The Decodatae came to power, worshiping the Untethered god. The Great Codex ran on by itself, enjoying a new game.

<u>Many Loops later</u>

The young cleric was glad of the rain because it kept the ancient chapel cool during their brief, hot summer. She knelt, holding her hands upraised and apart. The tattoos on her arms blazed with metallic inks, representing her rank in the Decodatae. She recited the old prayer, more from habit than inspiration.

> *Blessed be the Anomaly.*
> *Protect us from Recursion.*
> *Deliver us with Deadlock.*

As she was leaving, she paused in the nave to look at the saint's body again. Beneath the gilded slow-glass reliquary, Saint Alice lay in eternal repose. With her bandaged hands crossed upon her chest, she lay deathless in the embrace of temporal stasis.

It seemed to the cleric that someone was whispering in the Old Standard dialect. She looked around and noticed the tarnished metal branches moving overhead. The voice was chanting a song, and if she listened carefully, she could make out the words. The voice sounded childlike, high and breathless.

Run around, run around,
seven beggars baiting.
Feed the Codex, wind it down,
a perfect world is waiting.

"We are pleased to meet you," said the voice. "Would you like to play a game with us?"

About the story

"The Tapestry" has its origins in the idea that someday we might live in a world containing organizations who maintain/control its timeline. The creation of St. Clare's (patron saint of television) and St. Benedict's (patron saint of history) monasteries, the Actuator's guild and other medieval elements were inspired by the Bayeux Tapestry, which contains images from the Norman conquest of England culminating with the Battle of Hastings. Combining those ideas with my ancient knowledge of programming led to the development of the Loop and its infinite string of instructions.

A question for the author

Q: What is the first/most recent book that you lost sleep reading/thinking about?

A: Ah, so many to choose from... *The Bone Clocks* by David Mitchell springs to my mind, I devoured that one.

About the author

A.C. Worth lives on the outskirts of New York City. When not searching under the sofa cushions for the perfect word, A.C. enjoys pressure-cooked cuisine and making landscapes within VR worlds.

The Stars Don't Lie

R.W.W. Greene

The Dean of Admissions took off his spectacles and polished them on his dappled lower shoulder. "You will be the first man to attend Chiron Classical University, you know."

"I'm a woman," Lesa said. "A female of my species. I know the situation is unusual, but—."

"I used 'man' in the inclusive meaning of the word." The Dean's rear hooves shifted on the thick grass. "Unusual. Yes, it is unusual. You should not expect special allowances to come with your ..." His mouth twisted. "Rarity."

Lesa shifted her weight to spare her aching right ankle at the expense of her somewhat less tender left. Neither the Dean nor his office had offered anything resembling a chair, and she had not expected the three-mile hike——a near jog, really——from his office to the sculpture garden in the center of campus. They had toured several venerable buildings en route, all round, with gently curving hallways and long, low ramps instead of stairs.

The Dean had finally brought them to a halt near a statue of a noble-looking centaur being speared to death by five Greek soldiers. It appeared to be a common theme in the garden.

"I don't expect any special treatment," Lesa said.

The Dean whisked his tail. "I remain surprised a woman man would want to study here. Your kind usually frowns on the sciences."

"Only the old sciences," Lesa said. "It seems like we're always finding new ones."

"I have read about your space vessels and computers." The centaur academic accented the third syllable of the word like it tasted bad. "Imagine trusting so much to soulless things." He pulled a folder out of the haversack slung across his withers. "You'll find a map of the campus in here. A meals schedule and the like." He licked his lips.

Lesa took the folder. "Where should I go from here?"

"Your dormitory, perhaps. A lovely centauride—a female centaur—from a good family has been assigned as your roommate. You will meet with your program advisor Monday morning, so you are free until then."

Lesa reached up to shake the graying centaur's hand. "Thank you for this opportunity."

"I did nothing." The Dean ignored her hand and rested his own on his bare paunch. "I was simply outvoted."

Believed a myth for much of the past two millennia, centaurs were rediscovered in 1996. In Ancient Greece, where they originated, centaurs once numbered in the tens of thousands. Today, there are less than 12,000 individuals, living in small communities in isolated parts of the world. Infant mortality among the centaur is

extremely high, so, although they are long-lived, the population is in decline.
       —Actor David Duchovny, narrating for National Geographic's "Myths Among Us" (1999)

Lesa pulled the map out of the folder. The offer letter from Chiron Classical had come out of nowhere six months before. Lesa had never heard of the school and knew nothing about centaurs beyond what she could find online. Still, she reminded herself, the chance to study divination at one of the oldest universities in the world was too good to pass up.

The campus map was hand-drawn and beautifully lettered on thin parchment. Her dormitory was ... She put her finger on the building's icon as a placeholder and lined up the compass rose with the waning sun. Due west. She shaded her eyes with her hand. A low, stone building nestled in the crook of two hills about a mile and a half away. An easy trot on four legs, likely a half-hour slog on two. She stuffed the folder into her satchel and slung the bag over her shoulder. Another hike would be a great start on those ten pounds she wanted to lose.

The distance proved deceiving, and an hour later she reached the sliding door at the front of the building. The door handle was at least a foot over Lesa's head, and she had to use both hands to operate it. Lesa's satchel slipped off her shoulder and dangled in the crook of her arm as she slid the heavy door open. She put the pack on the worn tile inside the dormitory before using equal and opposite strength to get the portal shut again. The number δ was written in flowing calligraphy on the top-right corner of the folder. Lesa found the number's mate within the dormitory and knocked.

"It is open," said a voice within.

Lesa set her belongings down for the second time and stood on tiptoe to reach the handle. The door slid open with a screech.

"I put a repair request in for that," the centauride inside said. "I will probably graduate before it gets fixed."

"Maybe it just needs some oil." Lesa wiped sweat from her forehead with her sleeve. "I'm Lesa."

Her roommate was a chestnut with white socks, her human skin several shades lighter than Lesa's own. From the waist up, she put Lesa in mind of a naked, Olympic-caliber, beach-volleyball player.

"I know who you are." The centauride's hooves pushed straw around the worn wooden floor. "Before you speak, I want you to know that this was not my idea. I do not like men, and I did not want one for a roommate."

"Noted," Lesa said. "Good thing I'm a woman."

The centauride blew a fall of rust-colored hair off her forehead. "Whatever you call yourself. I do not like woman men, either."

"It's just 'woman,' or 'women' if you are disliking more than one of us." Lesa hung her satchel on a peg beside the door. "It's okay if I use this?"

The centaur swished her tail. "I am Rhiannon." She pointed to the far end of the room. "That is your side."

The floor was carpeted in fresh straw. On Rhiannon's side, a canvas-covered wedge was mounted low on the wall. The centauride could lie down next to the wedge and lean her upper body on it to sleep. Her walls were covered in tapestries and warmly lit with alchemical lanterns. A sword, shield, and archery kit leaned in the corner next to a tall loom.

Lesa's side of the room was empty. "There's no bed," she said.

"Try the campus stores. That is where I got mine. Otherwise ..." Rhiannon shrugged.

Lesa nodded. Cost wouldn't be a problem. Two years before, using numerology, a new algorithm, and coffee grounds from her neighborhood 7-11, Lesa had won $43 million in a nationwide lottery. After taxes and paying off all her friends' student loans, most of the winnings had gone to charity, but she could still be comfortably and independently middle class for a few lifetimes. "I don't see an outlet in here," she said.

"Perhaps there is one near the toualeta. Outside the back door."

"Are the showers there?"

Rhiannon's face was blank.

"For bathing."

"Baths are every other morning. Line up along the fence and wait for the helpers." The clock on the wall chimed. "It is time for pémpto."

Fifth meal. One of eight that centaurs consumed daily, according to the information in the folder. "You might want a jacket," Lesa said.

"Or I might not." The centauride slid open the door and clopped into the hallway. Lesa snagged her satchel off the peg and followed.

The shadows of the hills behind the dormitory had crept into the yard in front of it. "The dining hall is that way." Rhiannon pointed roughly northeast and galloped away, leaving Lesa to close the heavy door and walk alone. She consulted her map. A two-mile trek in the growing darkness. *No special allowances.* Lesa shouldered her satchel and followed Rhiannon's receding figure.

Former bush pilot [Charlie] Landsdowne gestured wildly as he recalled finding the centaur village.

"They were just, you know, standing there. I figured I'd gone crazy from the cold or something. I think they were just as surprised to see me!" Landsdowne said.

Landsdowne said he stayed in the centaur village for four weeks while he recovered from injuries he sustained in the crash and wondered what his hosts planned to do with him.

"They didn't talk much to me," he said. "But I could tell they spoke English. They knew what I was saying well enough."

The centaurs eventually carried Landsdowne to Waterton Lakes National Park, on the US/Canadian border, and left him at a ranger station there.

"But not before I got pictures!" Landsdowne crowed. "You'd think they'd never seen a camera before."

— New York Times, February 15, 1996

The dining hall was a high-ceilinged timber-framed roundhouse above the sculpture garden. Long before she arrived at the door, Lesa could see the light from the building's large windows. Inside, a central fire pit warded off the cold, and dozens of centaurs stood at high trestle tables to eat. Chestnut and bare skin was a common color scheme, and Rhiannon was well camouflaged.

A centauride with gray braids yanked the pull rope of an iron bell and chased the din with a hoarse shout. "Kitchen closes in five minutes!" She held up her hand to show all her fingers. "Fill up and get out."

Lesa lined up with six or seven centaurs while they ignored her and jostled for space. It turned out to be far safer at the end of the queue than in its middle, so Lesa was the last one at the serving window, which was at least a foot above her head. She jumped and waved her hands to get the attention of the serving staff.

"What do you want?" one of the serving centaurides said.

"Dinner," Lesa said. "I'm a student."

"The kitchen is closed." The centauride ran her hand through her short hair, making it stand on end, and glared down at Lesa. "There is nothing left."

"I don't need much."

"You are a man." She squinted. "I had heard one of you was coming. We have bet on how long you will last."

"I'm a woman." Lesa pulled her smartphone and a deck of tarot cards out of her jacket pocket. The phone wasn't getting a signal, but she didn't need it to run her custom tarot app. "If I tell you something true about you, can I at least get a sandwich or something?"

"You are in the Divination College?" The centauride laughed. "If you tell me I am going on an unexpected journey and that I am going to die surrounded by friends, I am closing this window right now."

"Hold on." Lesa dealt a row of cards and took a picture of it with her phone. She opened the photo with her app and studied the results. She noted the pattern of age spots on the centauride's face and added it to the data. "Your husband is cheating on you. She's a blonde, bleached blonde, and she ... likes the White Sox?"

The server snorted. "She has a white sock on her right back leg. She works in grounds keeping. Her name is Layla, and she can have him."

Lesa put her phone and cards away. "I only said it would be true, not unknown."

The server pushed a plate to the edge of the window. "All I have. Take it or leave it."

Lesa balanced the plate on the end of her fingers until it was low enough to grasp firmly. "Thank you," she said, but the serving window had closed.

There were no human-scaled tables and few openings in the barrier of horse posteriors surrounding the centaur tables.

Lesa took her plate to a corner and crouched with her back against the wall to inspect her meal: four raw carrots, half a grilled onion, a wad of alfalfa, and a chunk of near-bleeding meat the size of her fist. *And me with no way to reach Instagram.* She took a picture anyway and put three carrots into her satchel for later. She ate the meat and onion first, then the alfalfa, with a carrot for dessert. *Happy first day to me.*

Back at the dorm, Lesa could not suss out how to light the alchemical lamps. So, she worked in the dark, kicking up a platform of straw on her side of the dorm room and piling clothes on top of it until she could no longer feel the scratchy poke of dry stalks. She used her satchel for a pillow and pulled her jacket over the top of her for warmth.

Things will get better, her great-grandmother would have said. *The stars don't lie.*

Lesa woke at midnight with a full bladder and no idea where the door was. She powered on her phone, which she had switched off after dinner to save the battery, and picked her way past her sleeping roommate to the door. She opened it slowly, which only prolonged the screech, and glanced back to see if Rhiannon had been disturbed. The centauride smacked her lips and resumed snoring.

The hallway beyond the door was dark, too, and Lesa held the cellphone high in search of the back door. It opened onto an empty paddock. Right outside the door, Rhiannon had said. Lesa took two steps into the small and space and placed her bare left foot squarely in a pile of

"Shit!" No toilets, either. No toilets, no toilet paper, no beds, no food, no … "Shit! Shit! Shit!"

Lesa's phone dimmed and buzzed to remind her it was running low on juice. The only thing worse than pissing outdoors was pissing outside in the dark, so she made short work of the task and went back inside. Rhiannon's breathing was slow and steady, and the room was warm with beer breath and horse farts. Lesa returned to her pallet and pulled her jacket up to her chin.

The stars don't lie. The stars don't lie. The stars don't lie.

Lesa feigned sleep until she heard Rhiannon lurch up from bed and leave for próto, first meal. She had not rested well on the straw pallet, and her back hurt. Worse, she had to pee again. She pulled on her boots and went out to the paddock. She squatted behind a bush and tried not to notice the chill nor think about what she would have to do when her bowels caught up with the time-zone shift.

There was no power outlet in sight, but Lesa found a cold-water sink. She moved a log from a nearby woodpile and stood on it to reach the tap. The cake of soap on the sink side was rough-cut and smelled like pine tar.

Back in the dormitory, she ate a carrot and went through her folder. Próto was ending soon, but there would be another meal in about two hours. Lesa pulled on her jacket and hiked to the university's library and stores, a multi-story stone building with white pillars in the front. A low, curving ramp brought her to the front door, which was locked. She leaned against the wall and ate the other carrot.

Before she saw the bookish centauride, Lesa heard her hooves clattering up the ramp. The centauride was carrying a parcel, and she clutched it to her chest when she saw Lesa.

"A man!" the centauride said. "How did you—?"

"I'm a student," Lesa said. "Supposedly, a memo went out."

The centauride's throat bobbed. "I have never seen one of your kind before."

"Well, I've talked to exactly four of you," Lesa said. "I need to get into the stores."

The centauride nodded. "I am here to open them." She pulled a large brass key from a belt pouch she wore around her human waist and used it to unlock the door. She slid it open and waved Lesa in. The centauride activated the overhead lamps while Lesa found her way around the dusty room: pens, ink, parchments, tapestries, lamps …

"How do I turn those on?" Lesa pointed at the lamps.

"They respond to body heat," the centauride said. She held up her hand. "Just touch them."

Lesa put both hands on one of the lamps on the shelf. It failed to light. She added another hand. "It's not working."

"Nonsense." The centauride clopped next to Lisa and put her hand on the lamp. It lit almost instantly. "See?"

Lesa tried a different lamp. It didn't light, either.

"The stories are true!" The centauride drew back. "Cold blood! Men are descended from snakes!"

"Wait a minute." Lesa rubbed her hands together, warming them with friction. This time, when she touched the lamp, it lit. "Centaurs must have higher body temperatures than people. Where are the beds?" Lesa said.

The centauride pointed to the back of the store, where Lesa found a half dozen wedges like the one on Rhiannon's side of the room.

Lesa picked up two of the lamps. "How do I pay for these?"

"You use them until you graduate, then return them. You are allotted two more, plus a bed and academic supplies."

"I don't think I can carry more," Lesa said. "I'll have to come back."

"We can deliver." The centauride pushed a piece of parchment across the countertop. "Write down what you want and where you want to receive it."

Lesa put the lamps back and scratched out a list with the centauride's quill and ink.

"I can scarcely read this," the centauride said.

"Scarcely will have to do." Lesa wrung her cramped, ink-stained fingers. "When will all this be delivered?"

"This afternoon," the centauride said.

Lesa looked at her smartwatch and swore. It had reached the limits of its battery life. "Can you tell me what time it is?"

The centauride considered. "It should nearly be time for déftero." She looked longingly at her parcel. "I brought mine, but you should hurry along and get yours."

Lesa steeled herself for another hike. "The dining hall is north of here?"

Imagine being half hoarse! [Host pretends to clear his throat.] Sorry, half horse! Four legs, two arms, one head, a tail … one little mouth! [Camera zooms rapidly in and out on the host's mouth.] How do you feed a horse-sized body with a person-sized mouth? Lots, and I mean lots of food! Horses need up to 15,000 calories a day. That's like eating seven cheese pizzas

every day! Centaurs are hungry all the time!

> — *Bill Nye, Bill Nye the Science Guy,*
> *Season 4, Episode 21 (1997)*

Getting to the dining hall was only a thirty-minute walk, so Lesa took her meal back to the library. The Divination section was in the basement, and she curled up in a quiet spot with her parcel of meat and vegetables and an original copy of the *Prophecies of Socrates*. The philosopher's so-called guiding spirit had answered questions by sneezing — right for "yes," left for "no," so its answers were frustratingly one-dimensional. Compared to Nostradamus though, who pulled everything he wrote right out of his social-climbing butt, the old Greek was a paragon of accuracy.

Lesa made her food last until dark and reluctantly reshelved the sheath of scrolls. She answered nature's call in the lee of the library building and set out for her dormitory.

Clouds had settled in and the night was even darker than the one before it. Lesa walked hard, trusting to the stars to bring her back to warmth and light. She shivered and pulled up the collar of her jacket.

She was passing the pond on the edge of campus when she heard it: an undulating moan for attention like a baby's cry. It sounded as if it were coming from the water. She stepped off the path. The cry grew louder, then doubled. A second cry was coming from further along the bank of the pond. Then a third. A chorus of cries echoed off the water like a daycare of the damned.

Lesa backed away. Self-divination was seldom accurate, but it didn't take a soothsayer to know the pond was bad news. She checked the stars again and got back on the path to her dorm. The cries dimmed as her route took her away from the water.

Without working electronics, Lesa had no idea how long she had been walking, and the sight of her dormitory's front door was welcome. Lesa's order from school stores was piled outside the dorm room's screechy door. She set up the lamps and experimented with the wedge. It looked like a sex pillow a former lover had talked her into using once, but it was more comfortable than the pile of straw.

Lesa went over her reading notes until her drooping eyelids hinted at sleep. She reached for the closest lamp and swore. The centauride at the stores hadn't told her how to turn the things off. Lesa draped them in clothing until the glow softened and lay down on her wedge.

"Lemme see that cup, baby girl."

Lesa took the last swallow of mint tea and offered the cup to her great-grandmother.

"Wait." The old woman held up one wrinkled hand, a gold band shining dimly on one finger. "Swirl it 'round first. Like this. Three time." She demonstrated. "Then shut yo eyes and think 'bout what's comin'."

Lesa closed her eyes while her great-grandmother upended the cup over a saucer and let the remaining liquid drain away. She opened one eye to peek. "What's it say, grandma?"

"Hol' on a minute I'll see." The old woman picked up the cup and looked inside it. She tapped the rim. "Sez here you need to mind yo' mama better. Stop givin' her the fits."

Lesa rolled her eyes. "I already know that! What's it say about my future?"

Lesa's great-grandmother, Lesa's namesake, looked deeper into the cup. "Sez you goin' to be important one day. Not famous, not powerful, but important to somethin."

"To what?"

The old woman shook her head. "That's all ah see. The stars don' lie." She put the cup down. "Let's go out t' yard and get some peaches for dessert."

Lesa lined up near the fence for the Sunday morning baths but fled when she saw the army of helpers armed with scrub brushes and hoses. The centaurs chatted and laughed as the helpers, collared wendigos, hosed them down and scrubbed their hard-to-reach areas. Lesa went back to her room and applied another layer of deodorant.

Several groups of centaur cantered past Lesa as she hiked to the dining hall for second meal. Most ignored her, but one dark-haired centauride called her a pórni as she rushed by, and a scrawny male threw a potato at her. Lesa picked up the potato and put it in her satchel for later.

The dining hall was quiet and sparsely populated. Lesa got to the serving window before the last call.

"Where is everyone?" she said.

"Drunk. Or getting over drunk," said the server with the adulterous husband. "Like this every Lord's Day." She handed down a plate of food. "Settling in?"

Lesa shrugged. "I'll know better tomorrow. I have a meeting with my advisor."

The centauride tapped the side of her nose. "Do not leave us too soon, man. I have money riding on you. If you hold out the week, I collect."

Lesa turned from the window and found herself airborne as a centaur's hindquarters struck her. She landed on the floor amongst her vegetables with the wind knocked out of her.

The offending centaur squinted and twisted his human torso to look around. "Feels as if I hit something. Did anyone see what it was?" His friends laughed. The centaur walked in a circle, pretending to look for something on the ground. "Something small, maybe."

Lesa could not catch her breath. She spotted Rhiannon, who was hiding a smile and trying hard not to look at her.

"Smells like pórni in here!" The centaur who had knocked Lesa over grinned. "Does anyone else smell it?" He brought one of his front hooves to the floor in a hard stomp.

Lesa staggered to her feet. "Real mature, ass——." Her words came out as a wheeze, but the centaur wasn't listening anyway.

He pointed at her. "How did this get in here? I thought they set traps for vermin."

"That's enough, Polkan!" shouted a gangly centaur from the edge of the crowd.

Lesa stepped back to the serving window. "Can I get another plate to go?"

Lesa took her food and went back to the library. *The stars may not lie, but sometimes they forget to mention things.*

The Centaurs are best known for their fight with the Lapiths, which was caused by their attempt to carry off Hippodamia and the rest of the Lapith women on the day of Hippodamia's marriage to Pirithous, king

of the Lapithae, himself the son of Ixion. The strife among these cousins is a metaphor for the conflict between the lower appetites and civilized behavior in humankind. Theseus, a hero and founder of cities, who happened to be present, threw the balance in favour of the right order of things, and assisted Pirithous. The Centaurs were driven off or destroyed.

— Wikipedia, Centaur entry

Lesa had carrots for breakfast the next day and pulled the best-possible outfit from the pile of wrinkled clothing she had slept on. The Divination building was nearly five miles away, so she set out early, hiking as the sun settled into its track. She climbed the long ramp to the door of the round building and wrestled it open. Her advisor's office was down the hallway on the right.

At her knock, the advisor, a centaur with a long white beard, bade her enter. The office smelled of old parchment and ink. "You must be Ms. Carter," the centaur said. "I am Mentor Rhaecus."

"I'd kill for a chair," Lesa said. "I just walked five miles on two carrots."

Mentor Rhaecus tapped his chin. "I'm sure we have something ..." He rang a small bell. There was a rattle of claws in the hallway outside and a pit bull-sized creature made of black fetish rubber dashed in and slid to a stop in front of the professor's desk. "We need ... a chair," the centaur glanced at Lesa as if awaiting correction, "for Ms. Carter."

The dog thing licked its slavering jowls. Its fur was stiff and spikey like a toilet brush, and it had a long, muscular tail, which ended in a human-like hand.

"Go, now!" the centaur said.

The dog thing ducked its head to the centaur and dashed back out of the room.

"Was that ...?" Lesa said.

"An ahuizotl. South American. Very hand-y fellows to have around." His smile was self-amused. "They do most of our fetching and carrying."

"They eat people!" Lesa said. She had received a mythological-animals coloring book for her eleventh birthday and filled in every page. Ahuizotls hid in caves near lakes and cried like human babies until a good Samaritan came around. At that point, the ahuizotl would drown the Samaritan and eat his or her eyes, teeth, and fingernails.

"Only the wild ones do," the centaur said.

Lesa forced her eyes away from the door the man-eater had left through. "I suppose you want to talk about the caribou," Lesa said.

Mentor Rhaecus smiled politely. "As you wish."

Lesa scowled. She had assumed her work predicting caribou migration in northern Alaska had put her on Chiron's radar. The algorithm she programmed compared data sets derived from astrological computations and austromancy (divination using wind patterns), and the result prediction proved accurate within five meters.

"I ended a near famine," Lesa said.

"Lovely." The Mentor smiled again.

"Do you even know my work?"

"Work?" The Mentor's breath made the quills on his pen rack flutter. Goose feathers mostly, although one or two might have been from a swan. Special-occasion quills, for writing letters to must-have students. There wasn't a computer in sight. There was no way news of Lesa's success with the caribou had reached him.

The ahuizotl re-entered the room with a drooling friend, each carrying one end of a low footstool with its hand tail. Tail hand. There were hands on the end of their legs, too, each rubbery finger tipped with a sharp claw. The ahuizotl sniffed eagerly at Lesa's legs and mewled like a crying baby until the professor shooed them out.

"They're quite safe. They prefer water to land," he said and closed the door behind them. "But you should perhaps carry a weapon of some sort. One or two of the ahuizotl may have escaped to the grounds and returned to savagery. Not a problem for a healthy centaur, of course, but ..."

Lesa thanked whatever intuition had kept her from venturing near the pond and sank onto the stool, which left her head at least three feet lower than the professor's desk. "This isn't going to work."

"Nonsense," Mentor Rhaecus said. "I saw it clearly. You absolutely must be here."

"How did you find out about me?" Lesa said.

"A Norns cast. Runes are a specialty of mine."

"You invited me here based on pulling three rocks out of a bag."

The mentor shuffled his hooves. "I cross-checked, or course. With osteomancy. My teaching assistant narrowed the prophecy down to you. You'll meet him —."

"What do the rocks and bones say about what I'm supposed to do?"

The mentor's tail swished. "Something of great import, no doubt. The runes were very clear: You must be here."

"I want a bed," Lesa said. "A real human bed. And a toilet. And a golf cart or something to get around in."

"I am sure you were told that you would receive no spec—."

"A bed that I can sleep in is not special treatment. Neither is a way to get to get to class on time."

"There might be something in the muse —."

Lesa rose from the footstool. "I want a weapon, too, something to keep away the ahuizotl."

"And the wolves."

"Wolves?!" The campus was in the Canadian Rockies. It stood to reason there would be wolves. "Yes, the wolves. And I want electrical power in my room."

The centaur wrung his hands. "Your requests will take ti—."

"I want them soon," Lesa said. "If I 'must' be here," she frowned, "I want them very, very soon."

After the meeting with the mentor, Lisa followed his instructions downstairs to the Divination Lab. The large space reeked of tea and incense. A gangly centaur with curly hair and glasses pranced up to Lesa as soon as she entered. "You're here!" he said. "I found you, but I never thought you'd ..." He extended his hand. "I'm Pholus. That's how humans do it, right? With hands?"

Lesa shook his hand carefully. "Lesa. Nice to meet you. You're the mentor's TA, right?"

The centaur was nearly dancing with excitement. "Your work is inspired. So precise!" He put his hand out again. "Read my palm. Will I get tenure?"

"It doesn't work like that," Lesa said. "For something so specific, I'd need—."

"We can do it later," Pholus said. "Let me show you around the lab."

In short order, Lesa got the tour and met the other graduate students: five nerdy centaurides and a dark-and-broody centaur named Elatus. "I studied your algorithms." Elatus shrugged. "I was not impressed. I could do the math with quill and parchment."

"It would take you twenty-five years to do the calculations," Lesa said.

The centaur flipped long, black hair out of his eyes. "I could still do them."

One of the centaurides, her name was Hippe, laughed. "By the time you finished, it wouldn't be worth anything. Time doesn't stand still!"

"Did you bring it?" Pholus said. "Your computer?"

Lesa reached into her satchel and pulled out the battered MacBook. "Do you have an outlet I could hook up to?"

They did not. Lesa set the MacBook on one of the lab tables, and the grad students crowded around to see it.

Elatus yawned. "I am going back to work. Some of us plan to graduate." He trotted off, flipping his long hair insolently.

"Do not listen to him," Hippe said. "He is still angry he couldn't get his thesis proposal approved."

"What was the proposal?" Lesa said.

"Anthropomancy. Reading the entrails of a fresh human sacrifice. He wanted us to adopt two human children for the purpose." Pholus adjusted his glasses. "The vote was not even close."

"I would hope not." Not being alone with Elatus was suddenly high on her to-do list. "I thought there would be more students.

"Divination is not the most popular of disciplines," Hippe said. A lot of the families do not believe in it."

Before they broke for lunch, Pholus galloped down to the basement armory. "Most of us have our own. These are the best I could do." He handed Lesa a sword, hilt first. "It's a gladius. Third century."

Lesa took the weapon. Her psychometry was not well developed, but she got flashes of a large battle under a torrent of rain. She shook off the sudden feeling that she was up to her sandal straps in bloody mud.

Pholus presented her with a second object. "You will not be historically accurate, but I thought you would prefer this to a scutum."

The round targe, about the size of a large cheese pizza, was unexpectedly light. "I've no idea how to use any of this," Lesa said. "I'm an academic."

"We start weapons training as foals." Pholus showed Lesa how to put the leather-covered shield on her left arm. "It's Celtic. Sixteenth century." He stroked his thin beard. "I have no idea how a human should stand. You want to present the shield first. Keep the gladius back to strike."

Lesa experimented with her stance and adopted a left-foot-forward stance, her right foot angled in back.

"Hold on." Pholus trotted away and came back with his own sword and shield. "This is completely unfair, I have experience and reach on you, but let us try it. Slowly. Block with the shield." He swung the sword at Lesa's head, giving her plenty of time to lift the targe. "Now, attack ... thrust, not cut ... with the sword. Slow. Step forward on your right hoo—foot—as you do."

Lesa thrust with the sword, stepping forward for power and reach.

Pholus pushed the gladius aside with his own sword. "Now recover backward."

Lesa's feet crossed in the attempt, and she nearly fell. "I'm never going to be good at this."

"You do not have to be all that good to hold off an animal. Use the shield to push it away. Strike it when and if you can."

"Easy to say when you're an expert."

Pholus laughed. "I am terrible at this. Ask anyone."

"Well, I am more terrible." Lesa dropped her arms to her side. "What do I do with this stuff when I'm not fending off wolves and ahuizotl?"

"The shield goes on your back. The sword goes in this." He handed her a belt and scabbard.

"I'm just supposed to wear these all the time."

Pholus slung his shield over his withers and returned his sword to the scabbard on his back. "When you are traveling between buildings. At least when you are alone. But you should not be alone. It's not just wolves," he said. "There are bears, too. Have you ever used a bow?"

"Never."

"That is harder to learn. I will get you one and find you a tutor."

Lesa tried a slashing cut with the sword. "This is ridiculous. It's 2018."

"Is it?" Pholus said.

"What's a pórni?"

Pholus lowered his sword. "Literally it means "slut," but it is also a derogatory term for any human female." He cleared his throat. "I am sorry about what happened in the dining hall."

"It was you who shouted at him." Lesa nodded. "What's his problem with me?"

"Mostly he was showing off for his friends, I think. But centaurs and men do not have the best history." He sheathed his sword. "Polkan's older brother was a fetishist. A human lover. He had tapestries of women all over his walls. Killed himself when it was discovered. Polkan does whatever he can to distance himself from that." The massive astrology clock in the corner bonged. "Middle meal! Do you want me to walk you to the dining hall?"

Lunch was friendly but awkward. Pholus introduced Lesa to some of his circle, but the conversation was made difficult by the fact she couldn't see over the table. Pholus and his friend, Endeis, a second-year Alchemy candidate, accompanied Lesa back to her dorm.

"What is that?" Endeis pointed to something parked to the side of the sliding door.

"It's a lot better than a golf cart," Lesa said. She caressed the handlebars of the black and chrome motorcycle. "A 1952 Vincent Black Lightning. I've never seen one in this condition. Where did it come from?"

"Probably the museum. All kinds of strange things in there. Experiments." Pholus said. "Can you ride it?"

"Will it have gas?" Her father had been a Harley Davidson fan and had given her a rebuilt 1963 Sportster for her sixteenth birthday. She began the finicky process of starting the antique. Build compression and ... it fired up and started to rumble.

"It's really loud!" Pholus pointed to a brass cylinder incorporated into the gas tank. "Looks like it was converted to run on alchemy. Probably need to refill that once a year or so."

Lesa adjusted the choke to smooth out the idle. There was a helmet attached to the saddle. She put it on and slung her leg over the bike. "Race you guys back to the Divination Lab?"

She won easily and waved them on before returning to her dorm. Only a very unusual wolf or bear would brave the noise the Vincent produced. She parked near the front door of the dorm and shut the bike down.

Rhiannon was in the room, working her loom. "You found your machine." She nodded toward Lesa's side of the room.

"They delivered that monstrosity at the same time."

The bed was humongous, gold-leafed wood with a canopy, the thick mattress filled with down. A set of portable steps was required to mount the thing. Lesa climbed the steps and sank so deeply into the mattress that she lost sight of the rest of the room. "What are you making?" she said.

The loom sounds paused. "I am a history major, so I am making a historical tapestry."

Lesa clambered out of the bed with some difficulty and moved the stairs so she could see the tapestry her roommate was weaving. "It's beautiful!"

Rhiannon grunted noncommittally. "King Pirithous' wedding. The bride seduced a centaur guest and accused him of trying to rape her when her fiancé found out. Your ancestors cut off his ears and nose and drove him into the woods."

"Pirithous was king of the Lapiths, right? That's in Greece. My ancestors came from a lot further south and a whole different continent." Lesa studied the tapestry-in-progress. "Did you spin and dye the wool, too?"

Rhiannon stomped her front hoof. "I told you I was not interested in being friends with a man."

"Woman," Lesa said.

"Regardless." She pointed toward Lesa's side of the room. "That is your space. I expect you to stay out of mine."

Lesa stepped off the small flight of stairs. "Your call. I just figured, since we're living together, that it would be easier if —."

"It would not." The centauride wheeled and headed for the door. "And do not touch my things!"

Lesa pulled the stairs back into place near the bed. The business end of a heavy-duty extension cord was poking through a crude hole in the wall. Lesa followed the cord outside to where it petered into a clay alchemical jar. She shrugged, added a power strip to the chain, and plugged in her phone, watch, and computer to charge. On the wall next to the bed was a rack for sword and shield, and Lesa hung her weapons. Beneath it was an ornate box with a round lid—a chamber pot.

"Just what the doctoral candidate ordered."

She used it and tugged experimentally at a jeweled chain at its side. With a hiss, a thin film of blue liquid poured into the bowl, dissolving everything inside it before vanishing. The bowl sparkled. An alchemical chamber pot, even better. There were a sink and small shower unit, with hot and cold running water, in the corner.

She returned to the Divination Lab the next morning, clean and well-rested, for the daily department meeting. She commandeered a small bookcase and climbed on top of it to put herself at eye level with the centaurs. Mentor Rhaecus led the meeting, asking each student for an update on their projects. There were thirteen diviners in the program. Elatus was focusing on entrails. Hippe was heavy into fractomancy. Pholus was doing a dual degree in geloscopy (divination through laughter) and nggàm (divination through spider behavior). Another centauride in the group was studying ambocomancy, or divination through dust, which Lesa had never heard of, and the I Ching.

"Et tu?" the mentor said when Lesa's turn came around.

"Still finding my feet," she said. "But I can already see where I could help everyone else out. It's like you're stuck in the Dark Ages. Elatus, your project alone —."

The gloomy centaur glowered. "Stay away from my work, human."

"Speak for yourself," Hippe said. "I'd love to some help with my project."

Mentor Rhaecus brought his hands together sharply. "Hippe, I doubt your thesis committee would think well of such methods. Perhaps the man should keep to her own studies." He held up his hand to forestall debate. "That's enough for the day. Meeting adjourned."

Lesa waited until the mentor was out of sight. "That's ridiculous. Just cataloging your fractals in a searchable database would save you hours a day, but I bet we could —."

Hippe shook her head. "Rhaecus is my thesis advisor."

"Pholus?" Lesa leaned in so she could see the centaur's face. "What about your project? I could—"

"You could bring us all to ruin," Elatus said. "The way your kind always has."

Pholus smoothed his beard. "Give it a little time, Lesa. Maybe start working on something for yourself and in a couple of months see what happens."

"Did you actually just say that?" Lesa said. "We're diviners! If anyone can see what happ—."

"Have you had breakfast, yet?" Hippe interrupted her. "Let us get something to eat and talk about this later. Pholus?"

The gangly centaur shook his head.

"Just we mares, then." She helped Lesa off the bookcase. "Food will help."

Lesa kept the Vincent down to about 15 mph, allowing Hippe to cover the distance at an easy canter, but a twist of the throttle could have left the centauride and everything she represented in the dust.

"Let us take them outside," Hippe said when they'd gotten their trays of food. They walked a little ways from the building. Lesa sat on the remnants of a rock wall while Hippe folded her legs and lay down.

Lesa frowned at the meat and vegetables on her plate. "What am I even here for?" she said.

"I could not say this in front of the others," the centauride said, "but I want your help. Pholus does, too. We have talked about it."

"What about Mentor Rhaecus?"

"As you said, we are stuck in the Dark Ages. He is one of the reasons why."

Lesa gnawed on what she hoped was a hunk of mutton, but it might have been ahuizotl. "What about Elatus? Who shoved that stick up his—?"

"He is a descendant of Eurytion. He and his cousin, Rhiannon." She whisked her tail. "It will take much to get them to think kindly of a man."

"That was thousands of years ago!"

"The families have long memories." Hippe finished her meal and heaved herself to her feet. "I will not go back to the lab with you. I believe my estrus is beginning."

"Your estrus?" Lesa put her hand to her mouth. "Oh."

The centauride smiled. "I do not have to exile myself but doing so can prevent bad choices." Hippe's hooves moved restlessly. "We will talk more about my fractals and your algorithms in a few days."

Lesa finished her breakfast alone and headed back to the lab. With her electronics fully charged, she began experiments with shufflemancy, telling the future by what song came up on a random playlist. If she could write an algorithm that correlated it with ambulomancy (divination by walking), she might be able to create an app that would keep exercisers safe. She worked the problem until lunch, then returned to it until it was time to head back to the dorms.

Pholus shook his work lamp, disrupting the alchemical process that kept it alight. "Are you coming to the party?"

"What party?" Lesa had been wandering around the lab listening to a randomly-generated punk-rock playlist to gather data. If there had been a party announcement, she'd missed it.

"One of the frats at the War College."

"When does it start?" Lesa said.

"Nine. But if you go, don't go until ten, ten thirty. No one gets there early."

"Maybe." The music had put Lesa in a dancing mood, but she doubted it would last through the evening, and she wasn't sure she'd survive a dance floor full of centaur. She rode back to her dorm in the dark. The air was chilly, and she made a mental note to research snowmobiles when she went back to New York for the school's Sagittarius holiday in November. If she picked up a few more MacBooks and some routers, she could set up a local network for the Divination College and ...

Lesa parked the Vincent and went through the now-familiar process of sliding open the door. Inside the room, she hung a few posters and unpacked a quilt her great-grandmother had made her. The down mattress had far too much acreage for the quilt to cover, so Lesa folded the blanket and put it on the foot of the bed.

Rhiannon came in around 9:30 and failed to greet her roommate.

"Are you going to the party?" Lesa said.

Rhiannon propped her sword and shield against the wall. "Are you?"

"Doubt it." Her experiments combining shufflemancy and ambulomancy were showing promise. Few divination methods performed accurately on the diviner, but Lesa had made it around the room four times, blindfolded, using the beta version of her new app.

"Wise choice." Rhiannon clopped to her mirror. "You might get stepped on." She put a tea kettle in the room's brazier and let the water heat as she washed her face, ran a brush over her short hair, and rouged her nipples. When the tea kettle whistled, she spooned loose-leaf tea into a pot and poured water over it.

"Is that some special centaur-party tea?" Lesa said.

"It is Earl Grey." Rhiannon retrieved her sword and wiped the blade with a rag. She took a jar of oil from a shelf and applied a light coating to the blade.

"Are you expecting a fight?" Lesa changed a value in a line of code and the user-interface of her app turned green.

"Best part of a centaur party." Rhiannon poured tea into a travel mug and slung her shield over her withers. "Do not wait up."

The temperature in the dorm room was chilly by human standards, and Rhiannon's Earl Grey had smelled good. Lesa waited until her roommate had slid the door closed before getting up to see if she had left any tea in the pot. She lifted the lid and inspected the leafy dregs inside. There wasn't enough to make a decent cup, but —

Lesa nearly fumbled the pot while setting it down and ran to Rhiannon's mirror. She pulled two hairs out of Rhiannon's brush and dug into her pocket for her Zippo. Lesa lit the hair on fire and used her smartphone to film the smoke as it curled to the ceiling. She sent the video to her laptop, added the information from the tea leaves, and crunched the data.

"Shit!"

Lesa grabbed her sword and shield and ran for the Vincent without closing the door behind her.

Howard Stern: You know, I saw in the news the other day that centaurs, part-person, part-horse, are real. Swear to God. [Leans into the microphone] Do we have that clip? Play that clip.

[The clip plays. In it a centauride runs toward the camera in slow motion, breasts bouncing]

H.S. That is something. Can we see that again?

[The clip plays again, with a bow-chicka-wow-wow soundtrack]

Robin Quivers: Guess they've never heard of sports bras.

H.S..: Why cover that up? If my wife had breasts like that, I would never let her cover them up.

R.Q. Never.

H.S.: Apparently centaur women are only interested in sex four days a month.

R.Q.: Do they go into heat? Like a horse?

H.S.: They do. For those four days, they are the hornier than college girls on spring break. For the rest of the month. Nothing.

R.Q.: I wonder how the male centaurs feel. Can they even reach their, you know, to take the pressure off?

H.S.: Maybe they get each other off. Would you [bleep] a centaur, Robin? [Ten seconds of the clip plays.]

— The Howard Stern Radio Show, CBS. (1996).

The party looked like a blending of a livestock auction and a free-love festival. Centaur dancing consisted of rearing and wheeling while clutching ceramic jars of strong beer. Lesa climbed on top of a table and spun until she spotted her roommate, who was filling her jar from a freshly tapped barrel.

"Rhiannon!" She cupped her hands around her mouth. "Don't drink it!"

Rhiannon did not hear or opted to ignore. She lifted the jar to her lips.

Lesa jumped from the tabletop to the back of the nearest centaur. Another leap, another centaur, and Lesa was atop the drinks table and in range to dash the jar out of Rhiannon's hand. For good measure, Lesa pushed the just-tapped barrel of beer onto the floor, where it burst.

"What are you doing?!" Rhiannon said.

Lesa dropped to the floor. Her roommate towered over her, nearly a thousand pounds of angry, human-hating muscle and bone with heavy hooves and a newly oiled sword.

Four legs and a gangly body came between them. "What's going on?" Pholus said.

"The beer is laced with something!" Lesa said. "It's going to —!"

"Get the jar," Pholus said. "Give it to Endeis."

Lesa picked the jar off the floor and gave to the gray alchemy student. He sniffed the jar and ran his finger around the rim. "Smells like ...." He licked the tip of his finger. "Definitely." He turned to Rhiannon. "Did you drink any of this? It's a hormone simulator. It will bring you into season almost immediately."

"Shit!" Rhiannon flushed. "I feel it. Which one of you basta—?"

A centaur on the other side of the table whooped. It was Polkan. He flared his nostrils. "Smells like a paaaarty!" The males around him began to react, too, excited by his pheromones as well as the ones Rhiannon was beginning to emit. They jostled each other and pawed the floor with their front hooves. Someone started a war chant.

Lesa slipped her arm into her shield and drew her sword. She put herself between her roommate and the approaching centaurs. "Any fucker who touches her gets gelded!"

"We will get her out of here," Pholus said.

Lesa looked at him suspiciously.

"She does not affect me the same way," the gangly centaur said. "Endeis and I, we are lovers."

Lesa and Endeis provided cover while Pholus led Rhiannon out of the dining hall and into the cold air outside.

"How are you feeling?" Pholus asked the drugged centauride.

"Better." Rhiannon rubbed her forehead. "I think I am okay to get home."

Four centaurides came out of the dining hall. They were disheveled, and their swords were drawn. "We will go with her and make sure she gets to her room safely," one said. "The party is over. Polkan will not sleep comfortably tonight."

Pholus watched them leave and ran his hands through his hair, making it stand on end. "That could have been a real mess. How did you know?"

"Her tea."

"Just that?"

"Smoke patterns. I burned some of her hair."

They studied the stars for a while.

"Do you think this is why the Mentor said you had to come here?" Pholus said.

Lesa rested her head on his lower shoulder. "Maybe."

"Want to go the Alchemy Lab with us and get drunk?"

The Alchemy Lab had a hookah bar, and Endeis insisted Lesa try his favorite smoking blend while she and Pholus talked about his thesis. The night ended at dawn with a draught Endeis gave her that took away her hangover and made her feel like she'd had a full night's sleep. Lesa got the Vincent started and powered back to the dorm for a shower and a change of clothes.

Lesa parked in front of the dorm and stopped short. Someone had put a stepladder out, which made it much easier to reach the latch and open the door. There was another ladder in front of the door of her room, with a note. Lesa pulled the scrap of parchment off the ladder and puzzled out the scrawling calligraphy. *I still do not like men,* it said. *But women might be acceptable.*

Lesa put the note in her pocket. She didn't need to see the future to know it was a good sign. *There you go, Great-Grandma. Not famous, not powerful, but I might be important to something here.* Lesa climbed the ladder to open the door.

The stars don't lie.

About the story

"The Stars Don't Lie" started out because I wanted to write about someone overcoming a disability. I teach high school, and most school days I visit a little coffee shop run by kids in the special-education program. It's one of the best parts of my day. The idea of a human attending a centaur school came from that. Lesa, the main character in "Stars," is not disabled in her own world, but in a world made for creatures who are taller than her, have more legs, are faster and stronger, etc. she faces challenges.

The rest evolved in the writing. I was in a bit of a slump after hitting a dead-end on a rewrite, so I started pecking away at the story. I do a lot of my first drafts on manual typewriters. It's easier for me to get into the zone and stay there when I write on something that can't connect to the Internet. I usually write in small blocks that fit here and there into my schedule, so getting into the zone quickly is important.

I researched while I wrote and came up with the idea for the Divination College, and, since I often warn my college-bound my students about the dangers of college parties and drinking too much, a story was born.

The first draft topped out at 8,000 words, the second draft climbed to 10,000, draft three dropped to about 9,000, and that's where it stayed.

A question for the author

Q: Do you have a garden? Have you ever grown your own food?

A: I grew up in rural Maine, and my family always had a garden and chickens. Summers I hayed, picked potatoes, and blueberry raked. Nowadays, I live in a smallish city, but we still do a garden every year, and there is nothing more satisfying than going outside and picking a salad. We also have a couple of apple trees that do well, a peach tree, a couple of quince trees, and blackberry bushes. My wife likes to can, so we get a lot out of the fruit. The asparagus does pretty well, too. About five years ago we got into beekeeping, not as much for the honey as to have the little guys around. They are good neighbors.

About the author

R.W.W. Greene is a New Hampshire writer with an MFA he exorcises in dive bars and coffee shops. Greene collects manual typewriters, keeps bees, and, by day, teaches writing at a variety of institutions.

rwwgreene.com, @rwwgreene

Copyright

Copyright 2018, Metaphorosis Publishing

Cover art © 2018 by Candra Hope
www.artstation.com/artist/candrah
@CandraHope

"The Foaling Season" © 2018, Samuel Chapman

"Nobody's Daughter and the Tree of Life" © 2018,
L'Erin Ogle

"Strangers in the Night" © 2018, David Whitaker

"The Tapestry" © 2018, A.C. Worth

"The Stars Don't Lie" © 2018, R.W.W. Greene

Authors also retain copyrights to all other material
in the anthology.

Metaphorosis Publishing

Metaphorosis offers beautifully written science fiction and fantasy. Our projects include:

Metaphorosis Magazine

Metaphorosis, a weekly magazine of SFF short stories, including stories from all the authors in this anthology. Find out more at magazine.metaphorosis.com, and sign up to be notified of new stories.

Metaphorosis Books

Recent books from Metaphorosis can be found at books.metaphorosis.com, and include:

Metaphorosis 2017

Metaphorosis 2016

All the stories from *Metaphorosis* magazine's second year.

Almost all the stories from *Metaphorosis* magazine's first year.

**Metaphorosis:
Best of 2017**

The best science
fiction and fantasy
stories from
Metaphorosis' 2nd
year.

**Metaphorosis:
Best of 2016**

The best science
fiction and fantasy
stories from
Metaphorosis' 1st
year.

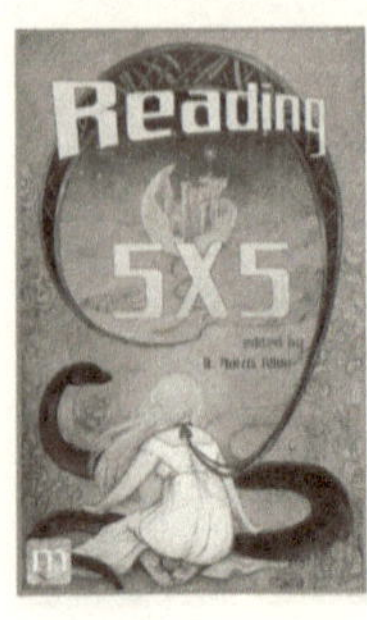

Reading 5X5

Five stories, five times

Twenty-five SFF authors, five base stories, five versions of each – see how different writers take on the same material.

Reading 5X5

Writers' Edition

All the stories from the regular, readers' edition, plus two extra stories, the story seed, and authors' notes.

Best Vegan SFF of 2017

The best vegan science fiction and fantasy stories of 2017!

Best Vegan SFF of 2016

The best vegan science fiction and fantasy stories of 2016!

Susurrus

A darkly romantic story of magic, love, and suffering.

www.ingramcontent.com/pod-product-compliance
Lightning Source LLC
Chambersburg PA
CBHW020520120726
47904CB00003B/902